SPY GEAR
ADVENTURES

THE QUANTUM QUANDARY

READ ALL THE

ADVENTURES

SPY GEAR
ADVENTURES

BOOK 3

THE QUANTUM QUANDARY

BY RICK BARBA

ALADDIN PAPERBACKS
New York London Toronto Sydney

ALADDIN PAPERBACKS
An imprint of Simon & Schuster Children's Publishing Division
1230 Avenue of the Americas, New York, NY 10020
Text copyright © 2006 by Wild Planet Toys, Inc.
Illustrations copyright © 2006 by Scott Fischer
Map of Carrolton copyright © 2006 by Eve Steccati
All rights reserved. Spy Gear and Wild Planet trademarks
are the property of Wild Planet Toys, Inc.
San Francisco, CA 94104
All rights reserved, including the right of reproduction
in whole or in part in any form.
ALADDIN PAPERBACKS and colophon are
trademarks of Simon & Schuster, Inc.
Designed by Tom Daly
The text of this book was set in Weiss.
Manufactured in the United States of America
First Aladdin Paperbacks edition June 2006
4 6 8 10 9 7 5 3
Library of Congress Control Number 2005927653
ISBN-13: 978-1-4169-0889-0
ISBN-10: 1-4169-0889-7

CONTENTS

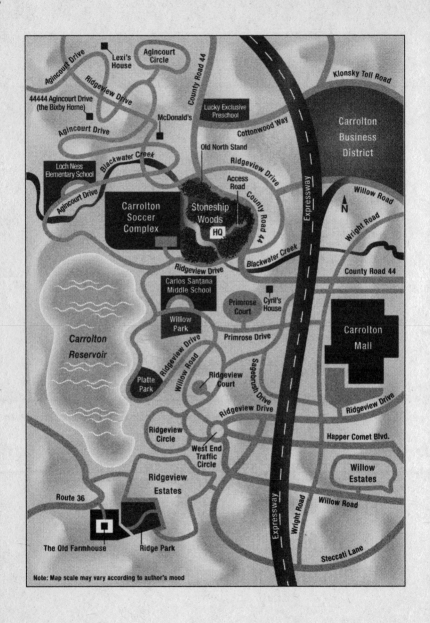

TEAM SPY GEAR

 JAKE BIXBY

 LUCAS BIXBY

 CYRIL WONG

LEXI LOPEZ

1

MALL MEAT

Holidays are good days for bad guys.

Bustle tends to hide criminal activity. In a town like Carrolton, for example, nobody's very vigilant in December. Life is too good. Nobody suspects foul intentions; nobody looks for evil. Shoppers simply rush past and don't notice you lurking.

People are too busy hauling huge bags of credit card debt from store to store.

Meanwhile, over in Willow Park, schoolboys in baggy sweatshirts yell and toss footballs. Vacation is almost here! Kids roll in the dormant grass, waiting for the first snow. They dream of Christmas loot.

What a bunch of happy, innocent fools.

Yes, life is good in Carrolton.

And high in the sky, sour eyes gaze down with disgust upon this Good Life.

For much the same reason, December is also a good month for espionage.

Good spies blend into the holiday bustle. Plus the trees are bare, so leaves no longer block your satellite spy-cam view, if you happen to have one handy. Fortunately, we do.

Let's zoom in on Carrolton.

Look! That big blue patch to the southwest is the Carrolton Reservoir. On warm days, folks swim and boat there. They throw sticks into the water that eager dogs chase. But it's too cold for water sports in December, isn't it? So let's pan our spy-cam due east. That's where the big holiday action is going down.

See it? Just across the expressway. That's the Carrolton Mall.

The Carrolton Mall is a "regional mall," which means it's so big that shoppers flock here from neighboring planets, but fortunately not the gas giants like Jupiter or the smell would be intolerable.[1]

The Mall Movieplex features forty "screening spaces" designed to resemble suburban living rooms except less

---

1. Parents, this is the obligatory gas joke, apparently required in every modern form of children's entertainment.

fake, and the Central Plaza features fifteen Eddie Bauer stores. To tell you the truth, I don't know what Eddie was thinking here.

Hundreds of stores, thousands of shoppers: an American paradise.

Naturally, with so much consumer action, you need parking, and lots of it. Sure enough, a quick pan to the south reveals a huge blacktop parking lot, big enough to bivouac the entire Army of the Potomoc. Look at all those people, scurrying about like ants! Now zoom in really close to the ground and check out the ants, scurrying about like people. Zoom back out. People or ants? Zoom in. Ants? People? Who knows? Out. In. Out. Keep doing this until you throw up.

Fun!

Hey, check out those two guys in blue lab coats, walking between parked cars.

Both carry take-out lunch bags from the Mall Food Court. Each wears a small headset plugged into a Black-Berry 7780, a slim handheld voice-com device clipped on the belt of the guy on the right, the tall fellow with gray hair pulled back in a ponytail. Also hanging from his belt is a security scan card with his picture and name: Dr. Matthew Smelvo.

Could these be high-level scientists on a wireless conference call?

They certainly look *dorky* enough.

Here's an idea. Point the listening dish of your Spy Supersonic Ear directly at them. Ah, now we can eavesdrop on their conversation.

"Look, Dr. Hork *invented* this field!" yells the ponytail guy, Dr. Smelvo, gesturing at his partner. "His work with trapped beryllium ions is Nobel quality, and I don't think ignorant meddling will—"

A response via the BlackBerry cuts him off. We can't hear it, of course, but both fellows look uncomfortable with what they're hearing in their headsets.

"But it's still too delicate," says Dr. Hork, a soft-looking bald fellow with a fleshy face. Unlike his angry companion, he speaks quietly. "Any interaction *whatsoever*—I'm talking a *vibration*, a *stray photon*—and the entire system collapses. The logic gate is unstable."

Do you understand what they're talking about? I don't either. Keep listening!

Now both scientists stop walking near a red late-model Subaru Forester.

Dr. Smelvo hacks out a sharp laugh. "Okay, so you want it in English? Try this: Our quantum prototype works for about twenty minutes. Then, you know, it *stops* working. Understand?"

Suddenly car doors slam nearby. The BlackBerry-wired scientists spin to face the sound.

Three large men step toward them from a white car labeled CARROLTON MALL SECURITY. They wear uniforms:

4

black pants, white shirt with a Mall Security patch over the breast pocket. Each also wears a Mauser M2 semi-automatic handgun in a Gould & Goodrich leather duty holster. Say, that's a lot of firepower for a security guard.

Now the scientists glance nervously at one another.

There is a long, uncomfortable silence as they listen to the BlackBerry.

Finally, Dr. Hork says, "Yes, yes, of course. But this little show of force is unnecessary, Viper. Your test will proceed as planned today. We didn't—" He gets cut off again.

(Wait. Did he just say *Viper*?)

Now Dr. Hork looks alarmed. "You land in seven minutes?" he asks. "Where?"

The response clearly agitates Dr. Smelvo. He shouts, "You idiot! You'll draw attention to the lab!"

Dr. Hork waves his fleshy hand to silence Smelvo and quickly cuts in. "Since you engineered your Firelight ruse, we've operated in *perfect* peace." He listens. "Yes, I know. The Agency believes it wiped out our regional activity by sealing the caves. We haven't seen one of their helicopters in weeks."

Smelvo can't hold back. He says, "The woods are *clear*, except for those stupid kids." He snorts in disgust. "Why can't you get rid of them? I thought you were some kind of mastermind."

The white-shirted guards quickly step forward to surround Dr. Smelvo.

As they do so, Dr. Hork says, "What do you mean? What *kind* of example?"

One guard reaches out and gently, almost daintily, plucks the headset off Dr. Smelvo's gray hair. He also unclips the BlackBerry from Smelvo's belt. The guard hands both items to Dr. Hork and nods respectfully.

Then the guards seize Smelvo's arms.

They drag him firmly to the Mall Security car. When Smelvo tries to struggle, a fourth guard emerges from the back of the car. He seizes Smelvo's ponytail and viciously yanks him down into the backseat.

Wow, let's zoom back out, okay? I don't like the looks of this.

Just a hunch, but I don't think those guys are actually mall security guards.

So what was *that* all about?

Outside, dusk creeps over the suburban streets. Dark clouds, perhaps bearing snow, hunker shoulder to shoulder across the horizon. Fortunately, *inside* the Carrolton Mall there is no gloom.

Zoom the spy-cam through that skylight on the mall roof.

See?

Strands of white lights twinkle everywhere. Holiday music wafts through the high cathedral spaces with its relentless urging: *Peace. Goodwill to men. All is calm. Buy stuff.*

Families meander down the polished wooden walkways, looking for holiday bargains, chatting with one another via cell phones. Nice Carrolton families. Normal families with normal kids.

But wait: *What's that, down there?*

Bobbing amid the mall herd is . . . a walking mop of hair!

Ha! Those of you familiar with Team Spy Gear will immediately recognize the Amazing Hair of Wong—Cyril Wong, to be precise.

Cyril moseys past storefronts with his arms stuffed elbow-deep into his huge pockets. He window-shops, seeking gift ideas for his parents and his best buddy, Jake Bixby. He stops at his favorite store, Absurd Image, to gaze at a display of hairless mannequins jumping unhappily on a glowing orange floor.

Next to him, a dark-eyed girl with short brown hair stares at the display too. She frowns.

"What *is* this?" she asks.

"Bald people escaping lava," says Cyril.

The girl narrows her eyes at him. "But what are they selling?" she asks, pointing at the display. "What's the product?"

Cyril glances at her. *Uh-oh.* She's pretty. He looks quickly away and nods for no apparent reason.

He says, "Okay!"

The girl frowns at him again. "What's your name?" she demands.

"Some call me Cyril," says Cyril. He shrugs, trying to act cool, which is difficult with hair of such magnitude. "I'm known around town as Cyril, for the most part." He fakes a yawn. "My friends usually refer to me as Cyril. Or just Cyril, for short."

The girl stares at him. "Your name is Cyril?"

"No."

The girl nods.

"Like, who the blazes are you?" asks Cyril in a bored tone.

"Cat," says the girl.

"You're a cat?"

"No, Cyril," she says. "My *name* is Cat."

"Cool," says Cyril. "Is that short for, like, Catalog?"

"No, it's short for Emily."

Cyril frowns, thinking. Then he says, "I'm deeply confused."

Cat shrugs and says, "Ask my parents."

"Why?" asks Cyril. "Do they know everything? Are they, like, the repository of all knowledge?"

"Yes."

Cyril almost laughs, but catches himself. With amazingly disciplined nonchalance, he yanks a wrist out of his pocket and glances at his XP-6 Spy Watch. It reads 4:15 P.M. In about an hour, Cyril plans to head home for dinner.

"Aren't hands weird?" he says, looking at his hand. "What if they weren't attached and you could, like, send them out on missions? Also, wouldn't it be cool if you had one on the top of your head?"

"Gotta go, man," says Cat. "See you later."

"Really? And how would that work?"

Cat whaps his arm. "You are, like, a complete donkey, Cyril." Then she turns and strolls away toward the Upper Middle Loge.

Cyril watches her as calmly as possible, putting his hand over the spot where Cat whapped his arm. He rubs it a little bit and grins. Then he turns and walks in the opposite direction—whistling.

Cyril doesn't notice he's being followed.

But *we* notice.

As Cyril passes a fitness equipment store called Good Guns! he notices a woman sitting on a bench, staring at her cell phone. She holds it to her ear and listens. Then with a fierce look, she leaps up and slings the device straight down at the ground. The phone shatters into tiny silver pieces.

Cyril stands next to her for a second, looking down at the pieces.

"You hit the floor dead on," says Cyril with admiration. "Very accurate."

The woman just stares at him with glassy eyes.

Cyril shrugs and moseys on.

As he moves farther down the Promenade, Cyril notices other cell phone users staring at their phones. Some look angry. Some look confused. One small girl tentatively raises her pink Cuddly phone to her ear. As she listens, her face contorts in fear.

"Weird," says Cyril.

Behind him, three murky figures continue to follow his footsteps.

Cyril veers into the food court area and makes a quick purchase at the Spicy Pretzel.

As he turns from the counter he catches a glimpse of someone ducking quickly behind a nearby pillar. Staring at the pillar, Cyril bites off a rubbery hunk of pretzel and chews.

He stops chewing. His eyes start to water.

Then he screams in pain.

"Fire in the hole!" screams Cyril, and he spits.

This expels a jalapeño pepper from his mouth. As it arcs through the air toward the pillar, it leaves a trail of smoke.

When the pepper hits the pillar, it explodes. Three boys leap out from behind, shouting in fright.

Cyril gasps.

Those are members of the Wolf Pack, a local gang of bullies. One of them is ringleader and mortal enemy Wilson Wills!

I'm a dead man, thinks Cyril.

Gripping his pretzel, he turns and pushes through the crowd at the food court. A quick glance over his shoulder confirms Cyril's worst fear—Wilson and the Wolf Pack are tracking him!

I need backup, he thinks.

Up ahead, the Grand Fountain rises amid a bank of escalators that funnel traffic to the mall's mezzanine and loge levels. Cyril hops aboard an escalator and whips out his cell phone. Then he speed-dials Jake Bixby's cell number. But when he puts the phone to his ear, he hears a recorded voice.

A pleasant female says, "I'm sorry. All FlexFone networks are currently down due to a national emergency of an undetermined nature. Prepare to stockpile goods and seek cover. Have a nice day!"

Cyril stares at his phone. At the top of the escalator he steps off and walks quickly. Behind him, Wilson and the Wolf Pack follow suit. Cyril tries to speed-dial his home number.

This time a recording of a deep male voice says:

"The National Weather Service has issued a tornado warning for central Carrolton. Doppler radar indicates a storm cell with funnel activity and dangerous cloud-to-ground lightning in your area, possibly right behind you. Seek cover immediately in an automobile, trailer home, tall tree, or metallic tower structure."

Cyril looks at the phone's display, examining the onscreen signal bar. Then, tentatively, he holds the phone to his ear again.

There is a pause. Suddenly the man's voice shouts, *"It's coming!"*

Spooked, Cyril jabs the End Call button. Then he looks up. This wing of the mall is a dead end. He stops and feels a constricted tingle of fear in his throat. Behind him, the Wolf Pack boys stop too. They lean with casual menace against a tree planter strung with suddenly ominous-looking holiday lights.

In a moment of blind panic Cyril considers hurling explosive jalapeños at them, but he manages to gather his wits.

This is a public place, he thinks. Surely not even the Wolf Pack would descend upon him here.

Or would they?

Now Wilson and the wolves move forward. The gleam in their eyes is chilling and carnivorous.

Cyril reaches into another pocket. He pulls out a sleek walkie-talkie headset—an earphone with a slim silver mouthpiece—which he hooks quickly over his right ear. A wire runs from the hands-free headset down to a Spy Link base unit attached to Cyril's belt. He reaches down and turns it on.

"Breaker, breaker, Hotel Quebec," calls Cyril. "Do you read me, over?"

He hears raw crackling static in his ear.

"Calling Hotel Quebec," calls Cyril, more insistently. "Hotel Quebec. Do you read me, over?"

Static. Crackling.

"Hotel Quebec, Hotel Quebec, I've got bogies on my six," says Cyril, glancing across the plaza at the Wolf Pack's approach. "I count three, repeat, three bogies, coming in for the kill, over?"

Seconds go by.

No response.

"Yo, Bixbys!" shouts Cyril. "Guys? *Are you there?*"

Nothing.

Trapped, Cyril looks up at the nearest storefront, the Ground Sausage. "How ironic," he whispers to himself.

Cyril walks into the meat store.

The Wolf Pack follows.

2

A ROLL OF THE DICE

Lucas Bixby, eleven, slams violently into the Stoneship warehouse wall and drops. As he hits the concrete floor, his breath expels in a loud grunt. Desperately, he makes a final lunge at the attacker.

"No!" he shrieks. "*No!*"

"Suffer, Bixby!" laughs the attacker, who cocks his right leg for one last brutal kick. Lucas tries to dive, but it's too late.

"*Aaaaaaaaaaa!*" howls Lucas.

A soccer ball sails past him.

It strikes a rectangular shipping pallet leaning against the interior wall.

"*Goal!*" shouts the attacker.

The attacker yanks the front of his shirt up over his

head. He runs in circles around the warehouse floor with his arms sticking out like an airplane.

"Serious foul!" yells Lucas.

"No way!" shouts the attacker, who resembles Lucas, only bigger, although right now you can't tell because of the shirt over his head. "Totally legal."

Lucas leaps to his feet.

"You're going down, Jake," he says.

The Bixby brothers, Jake and Lucas, sometimes show their brotherly love for each other in a way that brothers often do—aggressively, with lots of taunting and trash talk. Right now, for example, as Jake Bixby runs around gloating, Lucas Bixby gets a devilish smile and jabs out a leg.

Jake, thirteen, blinded by uncharacteristic vanity and more specifically, his shirt, trips over the jutting foot.

"*Aaaaaaagggbbb!*" he screams.

As Jake flies through the air, the shirt slips off his head. Falling, he reaches out and, with a lucky snag, hooks a finger through a belt loop on Lucas's pants. The pants jerk downward hard, revealing fluorescent orange boxer shorts.

Jake rolls across the floor.

Then he starts laughing hysterically. He points at Lucas and hoots loudly. "Nice trou!" he howls.

As Lucas hikes his pants back up, he notices that the

ball has settled near his feet. With a quick left-footed flick, he propels it toward another shipping pallet leaning on the opposite wall. It strikes with a forceful thud. (These pallets both happen to be twenty-four feet wide by eight feet tall, which coincidentally are the official dimensions of a regulation soccer goal.)

"And *that*, ladies and gentlemen, would be the match equalizer!" yells Lucas, bending down into Jake's face. "*Oh* yeah! *Oh* yeah! What now? What now?"

Jake reaches up and grabs Lucas, dragging him to the ground. Howling like wild beasts, they grapple until Lucas suddenly sits bolt upright.

"Uh-oh," he says.

"What?" says Jake.

"Listen!"

They listen. So does the author, not to mention millions, perhaps billions of readers.

Hear it?

An electronic siren wails in the raised control room suspended over a corner of the warehouse's main floor. The sound is dampened by the control room's heavy plate-glass windows.

Jake scrambles to his feet. "That's the Lazer Tripwire alarm," he says.

"Someone's coming," says Lucas, standing too. He gives Jake a look.

Jake nods. He says, "And it's an *unauthorized* approach."

Both boys sprint to a series of rungs recessed in the far wall. They climb up like rabid monkeys through a hatch into the control room.

Cyril is breathing so hard that his nose hums.

He veers toward the back of the Ground Sausage, where a young female clerk oversees an artfully arranged glass display case—meaty bins filled with colorful chorizo, salami, braunschweiger, and other mounds of chopped animal flesh seasoned and stuffed into edible casings.

Glancing back at his followers, Cyril approaches the clerk.

"That's some fine sausage you've got there," he says, nodding at the display.

"Yes, well, *whatever!*" she says brightly.

Cyril surveys the rest of the store. No customers! Across the aisle, Wilson and his cronies block the only exit. Trapped again!

"Too bad more people aren't here, seeking chopped meats and milling about in large groups," says Cyril. He turns to the girl, who wears a nametag that says, HI, I'M MANDY! "Are you working alone? I mean, like, no offense, but you're amazingly small and delicate, you know, for a human being." Cyril rises up on his toes and leans forward to peek behind the counter. "And unarmed as well, it appears. Dang!" The girl just stares at him. Cyril waves a hand in front of her face. "Hello?"

he says. "Are you with me, Mandy? Turn on the light, girl."

"Whatever!" she says, smiling like something very empty. "Can I help you?"

"Yes," says Cyril. "You can call the Homicide Squad. Just dial 911."

"Why?"

"Because shortly, I'll be some of that," he says, pointing at the sausage display.

"Did you wish to purchase a smoked meat, sir?" she asks, following some insane script in her mind.

Near the door, the Wolf Pack waits. Clearly they won't make a kill with a witness present, although Mandy barely qualifies as a "witness" in any normal sense of the word.

Cyril thinks fast. He decides to stall, hoping a customer or two might wander in. He looks at Mandy and says, "Do you have any unusual sausages around here? Like, sausage made from unusual animals or perhaps even insects?" He wipes sweat from his eyes. "Say, rhino or lemur or, like, like, heh, bats?" He points at some particularly pink, plump sausage links. "Betty!" he shouts. "That's my great-aunt Betty!"

The girl retreats toward a swinging metal door.

"I'll have to ask the assistant slaughter technician," she says.

"No!" shouts Cyril. "No, wait! Don't go! Don't—!"

Too late. The girl backs out of the room. Silence reigns, except for the bleak, rusty *creak* of the swinging door. Involuntarily, Cyril smiles. He turns to see Wilson strolling casually toward him.

The bully nods at a crate of meat. "Blood sausage," he says. He smiles. Fangs!

Cyril swallows and backs around the main display case. But as he rounds the counter, he finds his way blocked by a tall shelf stuffed with bratwurst links.

Wilson steps around the counter corner. His two minions step up behind him. Wilson reaches out and seizes a few strands of Cyril's hair with his thumb and forefinger, then yanks hard. As the hairs tear from his scalp, Cyril yelps. The pain is intense. Tears well up.

Then Wilson looks Cyril right in the eyes.

He says, "What's in the woods?"

Cyril licks his dry lips and says, "What woods?"

"Stoneship Woods," says Wilson. "What's in there?"

"How would I know?"

"You go in there every day," whispers Wilson. "You and the [censored] Bixbys." He leans closer. Cyril can smell his canine breath. "So what's in the woods, Wong? What's so interesting?"

"Well, trees?" says Cyril, voice shaking. "Trees, yes. Lots of various trees. They're everywhere. Left, right." He nods. "Some are tall."

Wilson grabs a larger clump of Cyril's hair. The bully

doesn't see the fierce dark eyes glaring at him through the bratwurst case.

"What's in the woods?" says Wilson with sadistic calm. He gives Cyril's hair another yank.

"Ahhhhh, well," blurts Cyril, "right now, there's a lot of leaves on the ground, *ow!* And, and, we've logged a considerable amount of squirrel activity by various, *ouch*, indigenous, *ouch*!"

Cyril's head twists sideways as Wilson slowly pulls downward on the clump of hair. But then Cyril notices Wilson's two companions. Both boys stare to their right, toward the main display case.

"Uh, Wilson," says one.

The other says, *"Wilson!"*

Wilson turns his head. "What?" he says, irritated. "Can't you see I'm busy tormenting someone far weaker than me?"

"Big," says one of the boys. He points. "Big, bad."

Wilson releases Cyril's hair and leans back to look around the bratwurst case. As he does, the store reverberates with a loud, sickening *thunk!* All four boys jump at the sound.

A deep voice growls, "I need more *mammal guts* for my new batch of blood sausage."

Cyril's eyebrows rise in recognition. He peeks through the glass of the bratwurst case.

A huge meat cleaver now juts from a wooden cutting

board behind the main display counter. Gripping the handle is a big, hairy hand. It wrenches the cleaver from the wood and wields it high.

"I prefer organs and viscera from the upper thoracic cavity," says the deep voice. *"But I'll take whatever I can get!"*

Wilson's pack flees howling before Cyril can say *Boo!* He grins and steps up to the counter. There, a large fellow in a bloodstained apron lowers the meat cleaver. A wild tangle of dreadlocks is wrapped tight in a hairnet.

"Marco," says Cyril. He looks around. "You *work* here?" He glances toward the swinging door. "Mandy isn't sausage now, is she?"

"Look, I'm busy," says Marco. He doesn't look happy.

"Doing what?"

Marco doesn't answer. He drops the cleaver and rips off the bloody apron.

"Come on, tell me," chirps Cyril, giddy to be alive right now. "Or will the sight of lunch meat sicken me for the rest of my life?"

Marco stares at him. Finally, he says, "I was using the store computer."

"Why?"

"Something very bad is going down."

"Where?"

"Everywhere."

Cyril frowns. Then he remembers his cell phone. He

pulls it out. "My phone system is goofy," he says. "Is that it?"

Marco's look is dark. He says, "It's worse than that."

"Worse?"

Marco lifts a hinged section of the counter and steps out into the store. Then, with unusual energy, he heads out into the mall.

"Let's go," he calls back to Cyril.

"Where?"

Marco is moving fast, ripping the hairnet off his wild thatch of dreadlocks.

"Stoneship," he says.

Stoneship's control room is a state-of-the-art spy center. Lucas Bixby sits in a leather captain's chair at the main computer and communications console, clicking away with a mouse.

"I set up the Lazer Tripwire on the east perimeter," he says, "out where the old access road connects with County Road 44."

"Good spot for a tripwire system," nods Jake, standing next to the captain's chair. "It's usually pretty deserted along that road."

Lucas clicks through a series of live video surveillance feeds that appear on the console's five monitors—a big flat-panel center display with two smaller monitors on each side. Whoever rigged up this "warehouse" (and nobody knows who yet) also planted dozens of field Minicams around Stoneship Woods.

Lucas clicks a few more times. "Here! This feed looks over the tripwire area." He leans close to the central monitor. "You see anything?"

Jake stares at the screen.

"Nothing," he says. "Can you pan around?"

Lucas holds down the mouse button and drags the mouse left. Onscreen, the camera view pans left along County Road 44. Then Lucas zooms in on a blue Toyota Avalon parked at the edge of Stoneship Woods. A man sits in the car reading a newspaper.

"Hey, it's Mr. Latimer," says Lucas.

Jake nods with a short sigh of relief. Mr. Latimer has been lost in the twisting suburban streets of Carrolton for three years, looking for a way back to the expressway. In the meantime, he's become a sort of neighborhood watchdog. Neighbors keep him fed; in return, Mr. Latimer keeps an eye on things.

Lucas pans farther left along the road. He says, "Check out that black BMW on the left side." He zooms closer. "Hmmm. Looks unoccupied." He swivels the camera view back and forth and adds, "I don't see anybody on foot who might have activated the tripwire system, do you?"

"Nope," says Jake. "Pan right."

Lucas drags the camera view right. "Aha! There!" he says, pointing.

Onscreen, a dark-haired young girl skips like a wood sprite atop a split-rail fence along the road. She balances with ridiculous ease.

"It's Lexi!" says Lucas.

Jake frowns and says, "What's she doing on the east perimeter?" He watches closely as Lexi Lopex, eleven and Lucas Bixby's best friend, hops along the rail until she disappears from the camera's view. Then he adds, "And she's being followed."

Three larger boys move across the screen. Lucas clicks to zoom in the view.

"Crud! That's Brill Joseph and his motley crew!" says Lucas with concern. "Why in dog's heaven is he tracking Lexi?"

"I don't know," says Jake grimly. "But I hope she doesn't lead that jackal here."

Suddenly, a girl's voice calls out via the console speakers,

Uh, excuse me? Hello? Hello? Can anybody hear me?

Jake and Lucas exchange a look.

"It's Lexi via Spy Link channel," says Lucas. He checks a dial labeled VOX CHANNEL on the console. Then he grabs a microphone on a flexible desktop stand, pulls it to his mouth, and says, "Roger, Lima Lima, this is Hotel Quebec, we read you loud and clear. Ah, we've marked three bogies, incoming. Repeat, three bogies on your tail, tangos marked as Whiskey Papa, over."

What? says Lexi.

Jake rolls his eyes and grabs the mike. "Lexi, the Wolf Pack is following you."

Lexi laughs.

Sweet! she says.

Lucas frowns. He looks at Jake. "She sounds, kind of, I don't know . . . *unconcerned*, wouldn't you say?"

Jake grins. "That's because those brick-butt bozos couldn't track Lexi if they had bloodhounds and a police helicopter."

Lucas leans to the mike again. "Okay, roger that, Lima Lima, let's vector you in. Recommend evasive vector Niner Niner Seven. Shall we plot a recon waypoint and go to Code Bravo contingency, over?"

What? says Lexi.

Jake grabs the mike again. "Don't lead them in here, Lexi. Go around."

Lexi snorts. **Why would I do that?**

Jake grins again. "Good question."

"Lima Lima," says Lucas, "this is Hotel Quebec, do you request backup? We can rendezvous in the woods at Point Foxtrot."

No way!

"But you've got three bogies on your tail. That includes Brill, the Alpha Wolf himself."

I'll lose them in thirty seconds.

Lucas smiles. "Okay, Lima Lima. Keep the channel open."

Lexi's voice gets suddenly very low. Roger that, Hotel Quebec, she answers.

Both Bixbys burst out laughing. Then suddenly another voice blares through the speakers.

Calling Hotel Quebec, this is Charlie Whiskey, Hotel Quebec, do you read me, over?

"Hey, Cyril!" says Jake. "What up, dude?"

We've got a dire situation, says Cyril breathlessly.

"Roger, Charlie Whiskey," says Lucas. "Can you be more specific, over?"

No.

"Why?"

There is a pause. Then: Security reasons.

"Okay, roger that. Where are you?"

Approaching the west perimeter fence. We'll be in shortly. Marco's with me, over.

"Cool!" says Jake.

"Wow, Cyril *and* Marco," says Lucas. "That's a tremendous amount of hair approaching."

Yes, very funny, Hotel Quebec, replies Cyril. And so *clever*. But if I may be serious for a moment, Marco has some rather unsettling news to report.

"Roger, we'll meet you on the loading dock, over."

Roger that, out.

Jake looks over at his younger brother again. Then he notices something over in a corner of the control room. "What's that?" he says.

He walks over. Two small white objects sit atop a folded piece of paper. As he approaches, he sees that the objects are a pair of dice.

"Huh," he says. "Check this out, bro."

Lucas steps to Jake's side and says, "Hey, I've never seen this here before." He frowns at his brother. "And I've been over every inch of this place, believe me."

Jake nods. "So this is new? Like, just placed here recently?"

"Yeah," says Lucas. "Like, today."

The two dice seem carefully arranged. Each one is showing a single pip—a pair of ones. Jake reaches down and carefully slides the slip of paper from under the dice. He opens it up.

"The Omega symbol," he says. "But it's slashed out in red."

He shows the drawing to Lucas:

Ω

"That means 'no omega,' right?" says Lucas. "But what's *that* mean?"

"Hmmm," says Jake. He looks over at the Omega Link, which sits on the console desktop. "Something about the Omega Link, obviously."

"Like, maybe we shouldn't use it?" says Lucas.

"Or shouldn't believe it, maybe," says Jake.

"But why not?"

Jake shrugs. "I don't know." Then he glances down at

the dice again. "A pair of ones," he says. Then his eyes grow big. He turns to Lucas. "A pair of ones!"

Lucas shakes his head. "So?"

"Dude," says Jake. "When you throw a pair of ones in any dice game, what's it called?"

Lucas thinks a moment. Then it hits him, too. He turns to stare at his brother.

"*Snake eyes,*" he says.

3

BIG NEWS

Lexi Lopez, aka "Monkey Girl," swings through birch trees. Her branch-to-branch movement is so fluid it's like liquid mercury.

These birch trees form the eastern boundary of Stoneship Woods. The forest is insanely thick here; Lexi travels tree to tree without touching the ground. When she reaches a taller birch, she clambers upward to find an opening in the branches.

From this high vantage point, Lexi scans a narrow strip of meadow about fifty yards to the east. Its tall grasses border the woods. There, Brill Joseph and his two goons pace nervously along the tree line.

Brill takes a step toward the trees, but then hesitates. He blurts some angry, obscene words. From Lexi's perch, Brill sounds like a huge ugly lemur hacking up hairballs.

Frankly, he looks like one too, plus he stinks. Plus he's ugly. Plus his dad drives a stupid car. Ha!

Cuss away, lemur breath, thinks Lexi.

Then a vaguely familiar sound rumbles from the northwest.

Lexi turns to look.

She thinks, *I know that sound.*

She stares at a canopy of ancient trees: the Old North Stand, about twenty acres of old-growth forest with mixed fir, maple, oak, and alder trees, the last of its kind in the entire region. One dark cluster of majestic Douglas firs towers a full hundred feet taller than the rest of Stoneship Woods.

But what's that sound?

Up in the sky, engines whine, not loud but deep, powerful. Lexi spots a circle of multicolored lights glowing in low clouds just above the great trees. It looks like Christmas bulbs lit under a blanket of snow.

Lexi's eyes grow big, and her mouth drops open.

"It's back!" she says.

The Bixby brothers step out onto the Stoneship loading dock to meet Cyril and Marco. Cyril and Jake clasp hands, punch fists, and then snap fingers twice.

"What up, road dog?" says Jake.

"It is what it is."

"Sweet."

Cyril nods back grimly. "But the woods are alive," he says.

Jake squints. "Wait. Is that an urban code-phrase that I don't know yet?"

"No," says Cyril. "I'm referring to the weird noises."

"What weird noises?"

"The ones in the woods."

"Weird noises in the woods," says Jake. He glances over at Marco, who shrugs.

"Correct, yes," says Cyril. "Noises. In the woods. And, as I indicated previously, they are weird."

"I assume you checked them out," says Jake, grinning.

Cyril whirls to face the west perimeter fence, whips out a Spy Nightscope (supersweet night-vision binoculars) from his pocket, and does a quick scan of the trees along the fence line.

"Jake," he says, "since the first day we met at the Lucky Exclusive Preschool, have you *ever* known me to investigate a strange noise?" He adjusts the binocular viewing scope. "Like, *ever*?"

Jake thinks a moment. "No," he says.

"That's *your* job," says Cyril.

"Right," says Jake. "I forgot." He nods at Marco. "Hey Marco, long time no see."

"Whatever," says Marco.

"We've got some big news, and I mean *big*," says Cyril, still peering through the binoculars at the forest. "Hey, here comes Lexi."

Sure enough, Lexi nimbly sprints along the perimeter fence. The boys and Marco hop off the loading dock and walk around to the south yard, where Lexi scoots through a jagged hole in the fence.

Finally, Team Spy Gear is fully assembled. Whew! It's about time.

Individually, the four team members are good. Together, they're invincible—unless, of course, the bad guys deploy tactical bazooka squads. Then it gets tricky. But that almost never happens.

Lucas approaches Lexi as she sprints up. "So you managed to dodge Brill and the meatheads?" he asks.

"Oh yeah," she says, breathing hard.

"Where?"

"They stopped at the tree line," huffs Lexi. She shrugs. "They're cowards. Plus they're really slow."

Cyril overhears this and clears his throat. "Ahem, well, when it comes to Stoneship Woods," he says weakly, "we're *all* cowards."

It's a fact: Carrolton kids fear Stoneship Woods. One reason, of course, is its Burmese tusk rat population. These social, highly intelligent forest-dwelling rodents nest together in tree hives. The females are known for their lovely, lilting song. This soft musical cry is usually the last thing you hear just before about thirty rats latch onto your face.[2]

"Guys, I've got some really big news," pants Lexi.

"Wait!" says Cyril. "So do I!"

Lucas looks over at Jake and says, "Hey, we've got big news too."

"Mine is bigger," says Lexi.

"Okay, you go first," says Jake.

"No way!" shouts Cyril. "Mine is huge. It's massive. It's, like, *whoa!*"

"Pick me first!" shouts Lexi to Jake, waving her hand at him.

"No, me!"

"Pick me!"

"Guys," says Jake.

"Me! I'm bigger!"

"Me!"

"Me first!"

Nearby, Marco watches this with his arms folded. Finally, he reaches over and clamps a hand on Cyril's shoulder.

He says, "Stop, before you degrade yourself further."

Cyril stops jumping up and down. "Okay," he says.

---

2. Note that Burmese tusk rats eat face meat only.

Lexi quickly tells everyone about the landing lights in the clouds over the Old North Stand.

"Circular shape, you say?" asks Jake.

"Yes," says Lexi, "just like before."

Lucas gasps. "It's back!"

Quick review: According to Spy Gear Case File 002 (chronicled in Book Two of the Spy Gear Adventure series) the team recently confronted a bizarre flying craft—just a month ago, in fact, on the night before Halloween. This ship was circular and featured a distinctive ring of multicolored landing lights. Its existence is documented by official Spy Zoom Cam photos taken by Lucas Bixby during the brief encounter.

Cyril turns pale. "Lights over the Old North Stand," he says in a hushed tone. "So the stories are true."

Jake frowns at him. "*What* stories?"

"The mutilations and such."

Jake rolls his eyes. "Okay," he says.

"No, I'm not kidding," says Cyril. "You've heard about them, haven't you? The cattle?"

Jake puts his hands on his hips. "Cattle mutilation? In the woods?"

"Something like that," nods Cyril. "I think."

"Dude, all I've heard is that the Old North Stand is a federally protected habitat," says Jake. "Nobody is allowed in there."

Cyril raises his eyebrows big. "And just *why* do you

suppose that is?" he asks. "Jake, have you ever heard of Roswell, New Mexico? Area 51?"

"Of course he has," says Lucas protectively. "He plays videogames just like any other kid!"

"Wait, wait," says Jake, holding up his hands. "Cyril, are you suggesting the Old North Stand is some kind of secret government facility? Like, where they keep space guys?"

"Technically, they're not *guys*," says Cyril.

"Aliens," says Jake.

"And mutants," says Cyril. He turns to Marco. "Everybody always forgets about the mutants." He shakes his hair. "I don't get it. You know, it's not like they're insignificant."

Jake has to grin. "Cyril," he says. "Maybe the federal government actually wants to protect pristine old-growth forest and the rare habitats that exist in its ancient ecology."

Cyril starts laughing hysterically. When he finally regains control, he pats Jake's shoulder.

"They love people like you," he says.

Lexi punches Cyril in the arm. "So I win, right?" she says.

Cyril glares at Lexi. "Okay," he says. "So maybe that's, like, kind of biggish news."

"So what's *your* news?" she asks.

Cyril pats the top of her head. "My news is, I'm going

to name you Spunky," he says in a perky voice.

"So what's *your* news?" repeats Lexi.

"Okay, okay," says Cyril. "My news is, Marco says someone has access to the Holy Grail of Hacking."

Lucas's mouth drops open. "No way," he says.

Jake looks at his brother and says, "You *know* what he's talking about?"

Lucas just stares at Cyril. "Not possible. How could that be?"

"Hmmm, good question," says Cyril. He turns and extends a hand toward Marco. "Maybe *you* should field this one, professor."

Marco gives Cyril a dark, edgy look. But then he turns to face the other kids.

"I've been chatting with a few of my old buddies," he says. "Apparently, there's a lot of chatter about diamond-level security systems getting compromised. Somebody hacked into the Federal Reserve internal network. Other stories are floating around like that. Somebody is slicing through firewalls with impunity."

"Wow," says Lucas.

"But the weird thing is, they're not doing any real damage. Today, somebody tapped into FlexFone Wireless and uploaded some prank messages. Anyone using the network got a surprise when dialing a number."

Jake nods. "So what does that mean? What's the Holy Grail of Hacking?"

Marco pauses a moment. Then he says, "Somebody's gone quantum."

"No way!" says Lucas excitedly. "No way!"

"Can you tell us what that means?" asks Jake, looking confused.

"Quantum computing is molecular," says Marco. "It uses atomic ions instead of silicon chips to calculate and solve equations."

Lexi crinkles her nose. "So it's, like, really small?"

"More like really fast," says Marco.

"Really, really, really, really, really fast," says Cyril.

"How fast?" asks Jake.

"You want a freaky example?" says Marco.

"Will it scare me?"

"Yes, it will." Marco looks at Lexi. "You've done factoring in school, right? To factor the number four, you figure out all the pairs of numbers that multiply together to equal four."

"Four is easy," says Lexi. "Two times two is four, and one times four is four."

"Right," says Marco. "So the factors of four are one, two, and four."

"So?"

"So now imagine a number *two thousand digits long*," says Marco grimly. "Today, even the most powerful supercomputer in the world couldn't factor this huge number before the sun burns out. It would take billions of years!

But guess how fast a crude quantum computer the size of a shoebox could factor that number?"

"A thousand years?" guesses Jake.

Marco smiles and shakes his head no.

"A hundred?"

Marco says, "Try twenty-seven minutes."

Jake says, *"Whoa."*

"I've read about this," says Lucas. "Theoretically, you could create a quantum-based form of artificial intelligence that could rival human intelligence." He nods excitedly. "Or even surpass it."

"That's *whacked!*" says Lexi.

"Not really," says Marco. "Most of the people I know are idiots."

"So true," says Cyril. "But anyway, such a development is decades or probably even centuries away." He nods. "Far, far beyond the realm of current science." He deepens his voice. *"Or so we thought!"*

Jake frowns at Marco. He says, "So you're saying that someone with even a small quantum computer could break *any* code? He could hack into, like, anything, anywhere? Even the most secure system?"

"Anything with outside access via pass code." Marco nods. "Bank transactions. PIN numbers on credit cards. Stock trading. And then it gets scary. Military weapons systems. National security communications. Everything would be vulnerable. And I mean *everything*."

"Everything?" says Jake with sudden concern in his voice.

Marco nods. "Everything." He looks at Cyril. "A cell phone network, for example."

"Or worse," says Jake.

Marco gives him a look. "Worse?"

"Let's head up to the control room," says Jake. He glances at Lucas, then adds, "We have something to show you."

Up in the control room, Marco holds up the dice.

"Pretty obvious," he says.

"Yeah," says Jake. "Snake eyes. Clearly, it refers to Viper."

"And that's not all we got," says Lucas. He points at Jake, who holds up the note.

Jake says, "The dice were sitting on this."

Marco, Cyril, and Lexi examine the drawing.

"The Omega symbol," says Lexi.

"Right."

"A red slash through the Omega symbol," murmurs Cyril, staring at it. He suddenly looks nervous. "Wait," he says. His eyes grow big. "Holy Dog Star!"

Jake nods. "You get it now, don't you?" he says.

"Get what?" asks Lexi. "What does he get?"

Cyril looks at her and says, "*Everything* is vulnerable to a quantum computer hacker. Secure communication links. High level links. The highest level, even." He points at the note in Jake's hand. "That's a warning. Maybe the Omega Link—" He doesn't finish his sentence because the scary music that I'm imagining drowns him out.

Jake holds up the note again.

Everybody looks at the red slash through the symbol: *No Omega.*

Then something beeps.

All eyes turn to the control room console desk, where the Omega Link sits.

It beeps again.

WOLVES AT THE DOOR

The Omega Link beeps yet again. Cyril picks it up.

"Hello?" he says, speaking to the device. "Who's there?"

"Cyril, I don't think it actually hears you," says Lucas.

"How do you know?"

Lucas looks at the device. "Well, actually—I don't."

"Right," says Cyril. "Nobody knows anything *whatsoever* about this stupid thing." He turns the Omega Link display screen toward Lucas. "For all we know, it's a hot link to the alien mothership."

Suddenly, the link beeps again and three letters are typed on the screen:

O N S

Then, with a beep, they disappear.

Cyril flips it around to look. "Nothing!" he says.

"No, I saw three letters," says Lucas. He turns to the others. "Did you see them?"

"O, N, and S," says Lexi, nodding.

"Whew!" says Lucas. "I'm not hallucinating."

"Look!" shouts Cyril. "More!"

Sure enough, three more letters appear quickly onscreen, one after another:

L A B

Beep! And they disappear again.

"L, A, B!" says Cyril. "Lab? Does it refer to a lab?"

"What's ONS?" says Lucas.

"Directions?" suggests Cyril. "N and S could be north and south. But what direction starts with the letter O? Ohio?"

Lexi leans over the device. "Why are the messages disappearing so fast?" she asks, staring at the screen intently.

"Good question," says Jake. "Cyril, set it down so we all see it. Let's keep a—"

Another beep. This time a full message pops onto the screen, all at once:

BIT-STRING ERROR
SYSTEM UNDER ATTACK

"What does that mean?" asks Jake, turning to Marco.

"This link is compromised," says Marco. "My guess is, it's about to shut down."

Beep! The error message disappears. Then another message appears, one letter after another, but typed very fast:

L O O K   1 2   O C

Beep! It disappears again.

"Is somebody getting this?" shouts Cyril. He points at a legal pad on the console desk.

Lucas whips an XP-4 Spy Pen out of his jacket pocket, pulls the pad closer, and writes down: *ONS, LAB, LOOK 12 OC.* He looks over at Cyril and asks, "What was that error message again?"

"Wait!" says Jake. "Here's another one."

Now one single beep, and then another full message pops onto the display screen, followed by a long series of beeps:

Q ! E R R O R :   D A T A   N E T
S T R E A M   T E R M I N A T E D

After a few seconds, the Omega Link beeps one more time. Then the screen goes blank.

Silence.

"Wow," says Jake.

Marco's eyes almost glow beneath his dark, craggy brow as he turns to Jake.

"That," he says, "was a wizard war."

"A what?"

Marco jumps into the leather captain's chair and puts his fingers over the keyboard there. Before he types anything, he glances over at Cyril. "Mind if I use your stuff?" he asks.

"You're *asking* me?" Cyril shows his teeth. "Hacker's code of etiquette, eh?"

"That's right, hair boy."

"Ha!" laughs Cyril. "Look who's talking."

Marco almost smiles. "So do you mind?"

"Be my guest."

Marco's fingers start flying across the keys.

Jake frowns. He says, "Hey, Marco, what do you mean, a 'wizard war'?"

"You saw it," says Marco, typing with insane speed. "Someone tried to message you. Several attempts, looks like, with a few fragments slipping through. But something, or someone, fought back, corrupting the stream." He stops typing and turns to look at Jake with blazing eyes. "Then they killed the link."

"Or maybe it auto-destructed," says Lucas.

Marco shrugs. "Could be. But I doubt it."

Jake picks up the legal pad where Lucas jotted the

partial messages, then looks at Marco. "So you think somebody tried to send us a message, and somebody else cut it off?"

Marco nods.

"And now the Omega Link is dead," says Jake.

Marco nods again. "For now," he says.

Jake looks down at the legal pad. "Okay, team, let's figure this out." He glances at his watch. "We've still got some time until dinner."

His cell phone rings in his pocket.

"Or not," says Jake.

"Dogs alive," says Lucas. "Is that Mom?"

Jake pulls out his phone and checks the incoming number. "Yes," he says.

Cyril lies down on the floor. "Excellent," he says. "I needed a nap anyway."

"No, no," says Jake. "I can make this short."

"Right," says Cyril.

"Seriously, man, I can proceed fast."

"Dude, coastal erosion proceeds faster than your mom's phone calls." He closes his eyes. "I'm pretty sure I could mine iron ore and smelt it before you hang up."

"Really, I've got a new technique," says Jake. "Watch how quick I can say good-bye."

Cyril pushes some buttons on his digital watch. It beeps.

"Are you timing me?" says Jake, holding up his ringing cell phone.

"No, I'm setting a wake-up alarm."

Jake narrows his eyes. Then he finally punches his phone's answer button and says brightly, "Hi, Mom!"

Four decades later, Lexi and Lucas play cards in a corner of the control room. Cobwebs hang from them. Nearby, Marco taps away at the console keyboard. His white beard touches the ground.

On the floor, Cyril snores loudly.

Jake slumps in a corner, legs splayed out wide, phone to his ear. He looks as if disease has sapped his will to live.

"Yes, Mom, I know it's dark," he says in a monotone. "But you see, there was still daylight when this phone conversation began, which was quite some time ago, I believe."

He listens. Then his eyes pop open wide. He sits up excitedly.

"Is that the *home line* ringing?" he says. "No, no, no, go ahead, answer it, please. It might be important. It might be crucial. Or it might be Dad. Or, or, it might be somebody, who, I don't know, has . . . questions. Yes! That's it! Mom, it might be a confused caller with questions you could answer in painstaking detail!"

Cyril suddenly snorts inward, loudly. The piercing sound awakens him. He sits up.

"No, Mom," says Jake, cupping his hand over the

phone's mouthpiece. "That was Cyril. It has nothing to do with faulty gas valves or underground piping."

Cyril rubs his glazed eyes, smacking his lips loudly. He looks around, confused. "Where are my penguins?" he mumbles. "Did they leave?"

"Yes, we'll be home in minutes," Jake says quickly into the phone. "Yes, yes, love you too, uh-huh, yes, right, I know, I'll be careful, yes, right. Yes, of course." He rolls his eyes. "*Yes, I promise to look both ways.*"

He flips his phone shut.

Marco stops typing and looks at Jake. "But will you floss?" he asks.

Jake grins. "Let's roll on home, team," he says. He checks his watch. "Wow, it's *well* past dinnertime now."

Cyril stands up slowly, scratching his backside. "I feel I've aged," he says.

As Lexi scoops up playing cards, Lucas hops up and searches through the gadget shelf.

"We'll need these," he says. He grabs a pair of slick goggles with yellow lenses and tosses the unit to Jake. Words etched on its metallic power-pack read SPY NIGHT PATROL LISTENER.

"What are these?" asks Jake, pulling them over his head.

Lucas tosses goggles to Lexi and Cyril, too, then dons his own pair and flips a switch on the unit. Twin LED spotlights mounted on the left earpiece shoot beams of piercing blue light across the room.

"Night vision with a bonus," says Lucas. He reaches up and taps a microphone mounted on his right earpiece. "This mike is a listener pod."

"Cool!"

Lucas grabs a small earbud hanging by a wire from the pod and slips it into his ear; the others follow suit. He adds, "The pod amplifies sound, letting you hear stuff far away."

"Wow!" says Lexi, turning her head toward Marco across the room. "Marco, whisper something at me."

Marco faces her and whispers. Neither you nor I can hear what he's saying because, well, we're not wearing Spy Night Patrol Listener goggles, are we? Gee, that's too bad, because Lexi starts laughing hysterically. She laughs so hard, in fact, that she snorts milk right out of her nose! She's not actually *drinking* milk at the moment, so that makes it even more amazing and, you know, maybe we'd better move on now.

Team Spy Gear has been making almost daily trips to their HQ for three months now. But familiarity doesn't make Stoneship Woods any less spooky. With their goggle lights bobbing like blue fireflies, the team moves east along the old access road that runs from the warehouse out to County Road 44.

"We haven't been out here after dark in a while," says Lucas nervously, his breath visible in the December night air.

"Not since Halloween," says Jake.

Lexi turns her head from side to side, illuminating the surrounding trees with her goggles. "These things are sweet," she says.

"Yes," says Cyril without enthusiasm. "I particularly like the way the spotlights cast shadows that move and *hiss* at us as we walk."

Up ahead, Lucas stops to look around. "Hey, you guys hold up here," he says, moving forward again.

"Okay," says Jake. He jabs his hand forward. "Scout on, Lima Bravo."

Lucas continues along the old road. He approaches a section where a wide strip of asphalt has been torn out; there, a line of trees, recently planted, forms a dark phalanx across the road. On the other side lies County Road 44. Stopping, Lucas reaches up to his goggles and activates the listener pod. Then he turns his head side to side, scanning the tree line, listening.

"Uh-oh," he says.

He holds up his hand and backs up slowly to the group.

"Activate your mikes," he whispers.

The other team members flick on their listener pods and look at Lucas.

Very quietly, he says, "Hear that?"

Amplified by the pod mikes, Lucas's whisper sounds almost like a shriek to the others. They all watch him jab a finger toward the tree line.

Jake turns that way. Via his earbud, he hears branches rustling in the wind—and then he recognizes the sound of voices murmuring.

Next to him, Cyril whispers, "I knew it!"

"What?" asks Jake.

"The trees," hisses Cyril. "They're . . . *alive!*" He drops into a crouch, wrapping his arms around his bent legs.

"Cyril, what are you doing?" asks Jake, hands on his hips.

"Making myself a smaller target."

Everybody looks down at him for a few seconds. Then Lexi reaches down and pats his back. "Nobody can get you down there," she says.

Lucas kicks Cyril in the butt. "That's not the *trees* talking!" he says. "Listen again!"

They all listen some more. Then one voice rises loudly above the murmur.

"Spread out, you [censored] losers!" snarls the unmistakably foul voice of Brill Joseph. "*Nobody* leaves this forest without getting mauled by the Wolf Pack, got it?"

"I hate to say this, guys, but we've got to douse these goggle lights," says Jake, "or they'll spot us for sure."

As the LED spotlights blink off one by one, Jake glances with concern at the two younger kids. But Lucas looks calm, and Lexi appears as she always does in the face of danger: electrified, even euphoric. The worse the peril, the more fun Lexi seems to have.

And then there's Cyril.

"I can't walk," he says, shivering.

"Why not?" asks Jake.

"My legs," answers Cyril. "It's too dark."

Jake grabs his best buddy's shoulder. "You can do this," he says.

"Can I?" says Cyril, a little crazed. "Really? Well then, *let's go!*"

He tries to take a step and falls, collapsing into a jagged heap of bones and hair. Suddenly, the murmuring beyond the tree line begins again.

"Shhhh!" hisses Lucas. "Listen!"

Now they can hear the voice of the Wolf Pack's beta male, Wilson Wills. Other voices can be heard snarling too. Clearly, a sizable pack of carnivores now loiters just beyond the tree line.

Jake creeps quietly forward and listens. Brill's voice rises again. "Are you sure this is where they *exit*, too?" he asks loudly.

"Yeah," says Wilson. "We've been tracking them to this spot for days."

"They never come out anywhere else?" asks Brill.

"No."

Jake finds a small gap in the trees and risks a peek. He counts twelve, no, fourteen boys. He sneaks back to the team and reports.

"Bad odds," he whispers.

"Very, very bad," agrees Lucas.

"We need more intelligence," says Jake.

"Let's go," says Lucas.

As Jake leads the full team up to the tree line, Brill raises his voice again. "Just in case," says Brill, "we'll spread farther along the road. Groups of two. Call if you see anything moving in the trees." He sends one pair south with Wilson, then several groups north, and stays put with a partner.

"Dang," whispers Jake.

Cyril swallows hard. He whispers, "So he has brains in that stump on his shoulders after all."

"Plans?" asks Jake.

"I say we toss out a shank of raw meat to the north," says Cyril, pointing up the road. "Then we run south."

Jake snaps his fingers. "Not a bad idea!" he says.

Cyril frowns. "Wait," he says. He leans closer to Jake. "They could be vegetarian."

Jake ignores this and says, "Lexi."

"What?" she says happily.

"Can you work north through the trees and create some kind of diversion?"

"Like, snap!"

Jake grins. "Okay," he says. "Then we can break south and head to Cyril's house."

"Sweet scheme," nods Cyril. "My mom will gladly

drive you guys home, especially if I whine really loud."

Jake nods at him and then turns back to Lexi. "Don't get caught," he says.

"They're slugs," she says.

Across the swatch of meadow, Brill deploys his troops up and down the county road. As he sends off each pair, they slaver and roar like beasts drunk on bloodlust. Then they slink off into the cold, blood-darkened dusk-mists of Rude Oblivion.

Jake hears a sharp intake of breath. He turns to his brother. "You okay?"

"No," admits Lucas. "I'm scared, actually."

"I think Brill means business this time," agrees Jake.

Minutes later Lexi crouches on a tree branch overlooking County Road 44.

She looks up and down the road, gauging distances. Her position is halfway between two Wolf Pack pairs crouching in the high meadow grass along the Stoneship Woods tree line.

Then Lexi smiles. She cups her hands around her mouth. She takes a deep breath and gives the Wolf Pack call—a chilling, infamous call known only too well to Carrolton kids.

"*Ow ow ow, owooooooooooooooo!*" she howls.

Up and down the road, howls echo in reply.

* * *

Jake watches tensely as Brill's group snarls at the sound of Lexi's howl. Green eyes glowing, they snap their heads in unison to face the direction of the call. Then they start howling too. They lope on all fours up the road to the north.

"Let's go!" whispers Cyril. But as he tries to step forward, Jake grabs his collar. Cyril yelps.

Out on the road, howls erupt.

Uh-oh!

Just twenty yards away, across the meadow strip, Wilson and two other pack members—the trio that Brill deployed south—skid to a halt. They turn to stare at the spot where Jake, Lucas, and Cyril are hiding. All three raise their snouts and start sniffing. *Snort! Snort! Snort, snort!* What a gruesome sound.

Jake and Lucas prepare for a fight. But more howls suddenly erupt to the north, so Wilson and his companions reluctantly lope off in that direction.

"Now!" whispers Jake. *"Run!"*

The three boys burst from the trees and veer right, sprinting south down County Road 44 toward Cyril's house. It's just a quarter mile down the road, past Blackwater Creek and around the bend that curves east.

Behind them, the howling stops.

"Faster!" says Jake.

Lucas, panting wildly, gasps, "What about Lexi?"

Despite the tense situation, Jake laughs. He pants, "Do you . . . think they'll . . . *get* her?"

Lucas chortles breathlessly in response.

Just down the road, they pass a black BMW parked on the west shoulder.

Back at Stoneship HQ, Marco is deeply engrossed in his online activities.

But something catches his eye on one of the side monitors. He glances at the Minicam feed. It's a view of the south yard, just outside. Near the fence, a small orange glow reveals the face of a man—a dark man, wearing a dark hat.

Marco stands up, staring at the monitor.

The Dark Man starts coughing wildly, and angrily tosses down a cigarette. He stomps on it.

Marco grabs his backpack and heads for the ladder leading down to the warehouse floor.

5

CAT BURGLARS

Monday, December 3, 11:55 a.m.

Bells ring in the halls of Carlos Santana Middle School. The morning ends at last. Lunch period is next. In the band room, starving kids fall out of their chairs. Some crawl toward the door. Others just lie on the floor and moan.

Over in a corner, Cyril Wong tries to jam his trombone case into a crowded equipment locker.

Public school funding for the arts, even in a fine community like Carrolton, isn't so great. Thus the music program shares locker space with other departments. A tall, emaciated man approaches Cyril.

"Having trouble, Mr. Wong?" asks Mr. Kornky, the concert band director.

"No, sir," says Cyril. He gives his trombone case a

couple of roundhouse kicks. "I've almost got it in now, thanks."

"Here, try this." Mr. Kornky hands Cyril a rubber mallet.

Cyril starts hammering at stuff in the locker. Things shatter. Something cracks. Then Mr. Kornky and Cyril take turns ramming their shoulders into the trombone case. After a few tries it finally slides in.

"Thanks," says Cyril.

At a nearby locker, Jake Bixby jumps up and down on his tenor saxophone case, trying to wedge it between four cases of frozen sheep brains. Cyril walks toward his pal, stepping over dead kids who just couldn't open their lunch sacks in time.

"We sounded good today," says Cyril.

Jake closes his locker door. "Yes, I agree, despite the bassoons."

"Really? I didn't hear them."

"Exactly my point," says Jake.

Cyril looks across the room. "Ah, that's why!" he says, pointing at some starved corpses. "The bassoonists are all dead." He shakes his head sadly. "The school district really ought to have lunch period earlier in the day."

"Yeah, like, right after breakfast would be a good time."

Cyril nods. "Kids need food," he says.

Jake grins. "Let's go eat," he says.

Cyril glances across the room. "Hey, what's up over there?"

Over in a dark corner, several Wolf Pack minions gather around Brill Joseph. He bares his fangs to establish primal dominance, then hands out small yellow slips of paper, one to each minion. The minions read, nodding and whining, with the occasional yipping bark.

"Marching orders, no doubt," says Jake.

"Fiends," says Cyril.

Jake folds his arms. "Might be plans for infiltrating Stoneship."

Cyril nods grimly. "Yes, I'd give my right arm to read that communiqué," he says. "Or maybe *your* right arm." He nods. "Now that I think of it, your arm is better than mine. It would be a more valuable offer." He thinks for a second. "I'll toss in my appendix and any other vestigial organ that is largely useless from an evolutionary standpoint."

Jake looks at Cyril for a moment. Then he says, "What a guy."

"I'm a team player, Jake."

Suddenly Mr. Kornky starts clapping his withered, blue-veined hands together.

"Move *out* now, band people!" he shouts. "We have a lunch rehearsal for the winter musical coming in right after you."

The annual winter musical is a huge deal at Carlos Santana Middle School. This year Mr. Kornky is staging the Broadway version of *Donner Party!* Competition for roles is brutal. Mr. Kornky always deals with a lot of tears after he makes final cast selections. And once he gets the parents out of his office, the student rejects are pretty sad too.

Cyril and Jake start pushing through the incoming stream of students. Then Cyril sees a familiar face entering the room. He freezes.

"Cat!" he exclaims.

"Where?" asks Jake, looking down low. "Where is it?"

"Quick!" hisses Cyril. "This way."

Cyril grabs Jake's sleeve and yanks him up onto a small rehearsal stage, behind the main curtain.

"Is it dangerous?" asks Jake, confused. "Will it attack?"

Cyril, sweating, peeks out. "Dude, I didn't know she goes to Santana," he says.

"What the flip are you talking about?" asks Jake.

"That girl!"

Jake puts his eye to the curtain gap. "Which one?"

"There," points Cyril. "The one carrying the big cooking kettle."

"Short dark hair?"

"Yeah."

"Wow," says Jake. "She's hot."

"Too bad she, like, totally hates me," says Cyril with a weak laugh.

"How do you know?"

"She punched me at the mall."

Jakes eyes widen. "She *punched* you?"

"Yeah," says Cyril. "She whapped me pretty hard, like, right here." He points at his arm. "And then she called me a donkey."

Jake points at Cat. "*That* girl? She *hit* you?"

"Yes."

Jake's grin grows. He says, "Intense."

Cyril turns to watch Cat through the curtain. When he turns back, Jake is still grinning at him.

"What?" he asks.

"You sly goat," says Jake.

Cyril frowns and peeks through the curtain again. As Cat sings warm-up scales, she drops the kettle and starts swinging her arms in big circles. Then she steps up onto the stage.

Jake begins, "Maybe you should—"

"Shhhh!" hisses Cyril. *"She's coming this way!"*

Cyril watches Cat's approach so intently that he fails to notice Jake sliding over behind him. As Cat nears center stage, Jake puts his hands on Cyril's back and gives him a quick shove.

Cyril stumbles through the curtains. Cat stops cold and stares at him.

"Oh, hey, well," says Cyril, his voice cracking. "Yes. Great. And here I am."

"Cyril Wong," says Cat.

"Yes, hello, I didn't see you there, not until just now," says Cyril briskly, nodding. He turns back to the curtain and starts examining it with a professional air. "And yes, the curtain seems to work *just fine* now. I think we got it fixed, Bob."

Cat squints at him. "Bob?" she asks.

"Yes, Bob. My *business* associate."

Cyril rips the curtain open, revealing Jake.

Jake waves feebly at Cat. "Actually, I'm not Bob," he says.

"You're Jake Bixby," she says.

Cyril eyes her suspiciously. "How do you know our names?"

"You're *eighth* graders," says Cat. "Ever so much bigger than life." She stretches her arms side to side, loosening up for the dance rehearsal. "I'm just a lowly seventh grader myself."

"That's okay," says Jake. "We like you anyway." He glances sideways at Cyril.

Cat looks at Cyril too. "Is that so?"

Cyril squirms. "Knock it off, Bob," he murmurs.

Jake gives Cyril's shoulder a jovial slap. "You kids have fun," he says. Whistling, he saunters toward the band room doorway.

Cyril, stunned, watches him go. "He's leaving," he says.

"That Bob's a funny guy," says Cat, watching Jake exit the room.

"Yes, hilarious," says Cyril.

Cat and Cyril turn to face each other.

"Well?" says Cat.

Cyril shrugs. "Well what? What do you want from me?"

"Watch me rehearse this next scene," she says. "I could use some feedback."

Cyril squints. "What happens in it?"

"I eat my aunt and two cousins, then sing about how cold it is," she says. "It's called, 'There's Nothing Quite Like a Family Meal.'"

Cyril nods. "Cool," he says.

12:16 p.m. Marco trudges across the vast parking lot of the Carrolton Mall. His backpack sways from side to side, looking like huge, hunched shoulders. His dreadlocks flutter in a brisk December breeze.

He approaches a manned parking booth. Looking both ways, he slips inside.

The attendant spins around, surprised. But when he sees Marco, he grins.

"Dude!" says the attendant.

"Hey." Marco nods. He looks over the young

man's uniform. "I see you found a high-paying job too."

"I'm laying low," says the attendant.

Marco looks around the booth. "Yes, this is about as low as it gets."

"Get down!" says the attendant suddenly.

Marco ducks. He hears a vehicle approach the booth. Above him, the attendant waves the car through the parking gate. Marco peeks out the doorway. A white Mall Security car with dark-tinted windows trolls slowly past.

"Those guys are scary," says the attendant, eyeing the car. "They creep me out, man."

Marco watches the vehicle stop at the Mall Food Court entrance. A bald, fleshy man in a blue lab coat steps out of the car. The man looks around, and then hurries through the mall doors.

Two massive security guards exit the car too. They post themselves by the doors.

In the booth, Marco quickly strips off his backpack.

"Can I leave this here for a while?" he says urgently.

"No way, dude! This isn't a storage locker."

Marco pulls a fifty-dollar bill out of his pocket and jabs it at the attendant.

"I thought you were broke," says the attendant, grabbing the bill with a grin.

"I am."

"So where'd you get green?"

"You don't want to know."

Marco steps out of the booth, scans the lot, and crouches down. He takes a deep breath and murmurs to himself, "I hate this."

Marco starts scuttling sideways like a crab through parked cars, working his way toward the Mall Food Court entrance.

12:28 p.m. In the lunch room, Jake ducks under flying food and joins Lucas and Lexi at a corner table. He opens his lunch bag and pulls out a plastic container. A glutinous glob of yellow matter jiggles inside.

"Ah, Parmesan Jell-O," he says. "And Mom comes through again."

He jabs the container toward Lexi, who shrinks away in fright.

"Where's Cyril?" asks Lucas, chewing.

Jake gives his brother a sly look. "I believe Cyril's busy," he says.

"Doing what?"

"Drooling," says Jake. He checks his watch. "Right about now, he should be knocking over an entire row of music stands."

Lexi's eyes grow big. "Cyril's talking to a girl?"

Jake gives her an admiring look. "How did you know that?" he asks.

"A woman knows these things," says Lexi.

This remark causes the Bixbys to start hooting and whapping Lexi on the back. Lexi smiles and jams a huge chunk of fresh carrot into her mouth. Her crunching is so loud it revives corpses in Carrolton Cemetery, who rise from their graves and start moaning about taking revenge on the living.

Okay, maybe that sounds a bit fantastic.

But frankly, we think this phenomenon explains Lavina the Lunch Lady.

Lavina is the newest member of the cafeteria staff at Carlos Santana Middle School. She pushes around a wheeled wastebasket all day, cleaning off tables and scaring the bejabbers out of kids who make the mistake of looking her in the eye.

At this very moment Lavina picks up trash just two tables away from Team Spy Gear.

Lucas shades his eyes with a hand, trying not to meet her ghastly, repugnant gaze.

"Just don't look," says Lexi. "Is it so hard?"

Jake adds, "Have you no self-control?"

"No," says Lucas. "As a matter of fact, I don't."

Jake grins and says, "They say she turned Trevor Murch into a beanbag."

Lucas nods. "He's a comfortable guy."

With a grunt, Lavina slams her enormous hairy arm down onto a nearby table. Shock waves reverberate across the lunch room. Then she swipes her arm across the tabletop. Garbage cascades into her wastebasket.

"Okay, let's call this meeting to order," says Jake. "As I see it, we have two tasks of immediate importance." He points at Lucas, who stands up.

"Figure out what the Omega Link message fragments mean?" says Lucas.

"That's one," Jake says with a nod.

Lucas sits. Now Jake points at Lexi. She stands up.

"Spy on Cyril's new girlfriend?" she guesses.

"No."

Lexi thinks hard. "Spy on the Wolf Pack?"

"Why?" asks Jake.

"To see why they're following us everywhere?"

"That's two," says Jake. "You may sit." Then he frowns. "Actually, I have a third concern as well."

"Marco," says Lucas.

"Yeah," says Jake. "Why didn't he check in with us yesterday? I can't believe he hacked around all night Saturday and all day Sunday—and came up with *nothing* interesting to tell us."

"He's a weird guy," says Lexi.

"Big understatement," says Lucas.

Jake turns to Lexi. "Okay, Lucas and I went over the Omega fragments yesterday, and here's what we came up with." He nods at Lucas, who pulls a notepad out of his backpack. "We have a few pages of ideas on each fragment, but we were hoping that—"

"The hovercraft was over the Old, North, Stand," says Lexi. "O, N, S."

Jake's jaw drops. He exchanges a look with Lucas, who drops his notepad. Then he rips out two pages and wads them up. He grins at Lexi and tosses the wads at Lavina's trash can.

"Next clue," he says.

"L, A, B really could mean just what it spells," says Jake. "A laboratory."

"Considering what we found at Firelight, I wouldn't be surprised," agrees Lucas.

Quick review: Just one month ago, in the last Spy Gear Adventure (detailed in Book Two of this series), Team Spy Gear discovered and flooded the offices of a videogame design group known as Firelight Studios. This wiped out Firelight's computer servers for their highly popular online game entitled M3 (short for Massively Multiplayer Mystery). This was a good thing, because M3 was laced with subliminal fear-trigger messages affecting the behavior of players, including many kids in Carrolton.

Even more frightening, however, was the fact that Firelight Studios doubled as a breeding laboratory for nasty attack insects. Evidence suggested that the lab was the brainchild of a shadowy, unseen, evil mastermind known only as Viper.

"Do you think Viper has another lab hidden somewhere in the Old North Stand?" asks Lucas excitedly.

"It's a theory," Jake answers.

Lucas looks at Lexi. "Okay, hotshot," he says. He flips his notepad to another page. "What does *this* mean?" He points at the page, where a message fragment reads *LOOK 12 OC*.

Lexi shrugs. "I don't know," she says.

Lucas flips to several pages of scribbled notes in the notepad. "Well, we spent about an hour last night—"

"Look at twelve o'clock?" says Lexi.

Lucas freezes. He stares at Jake, who stares back with wide eyes.

"Look twelve OC," says Jake. "Of course."

"Wow," says Lucas. He rips several more pages out of his notebook and crumples them. "It makes sense, doesn't it?" Then he hops to his feet. He can't sit still anymore. He starts pacing and says, "So maybe there's a lab hidden in the Old North Stand, and the lab workers exit or enter at twelve o'clock?" He shakes his head. "Wow! Wow! But of course the question is *which* twelve o'clock? Are we talking about *noon* or *midnight*?"

"Good question," Jake agrees.

"Plus, how do we actually get into the Old North Stand to investigate?" continues Lucas with energy. "It's illegal to go in, right? Isn't the old-growth forest sealed off somehow?" He paces faster. "But if there's a laboratory, the lab people must get in and out somehow. There must be a secret passage, or, or, or maybe they *fly* in and out, yeah, maybe via that hovership with all the colored landing lights? Maybe *that's* it!"

"Log those thoughts, bro," says Jake.

Lucas nods and reaches into his book bag to pull out the official Team Spy Gear casebook. He whips it open and starts writing furiously. Lucas has been keeping meticulous case notes since the very first Spy Gear adventure.

Suddenly, Cyril plops down into the seat next to Jake. His smile is so big it wraps completely around his head, twice.

Jake raises his eyebrows. "So?" he asks.

"So, she hates the Wolf Pack," says Cyril.

"*Everybody* hates the Wolf Pack," says Jake.

"Yes," replies Cyril. "But she *really* hates the Wolf Pack." He leans back. "Wilson Wills is her cousin."

"What?" exclaims Jake.

Kids, spies usually stay hidden. They sneak around and stay low and peek and eavesdrop.

But sometimes when you're a spy, you spy right out in the open. Your job: Pretend to be someone else. This is called covert undercover work. It's a dangerous assignment, and only the very best spies can pull it off.

Picture it: You walk right up to the bad guys and act

innocent, then try to overhear their evil plans. Better yet, you pretend to be a bad guy yourself and join in the actual plotting.

The very thought of such daring pretense makes the author queasy and gives him the heebie-jeebies.[3]

"Who is this *she* you speak of?" shouts Lucas, hopping on one foot. "Who in the name of the Blue Monkey Gods are we talking about?"

Cyril points across the lunchroom.

The others turn to see Wilson and other Wolf Pack boys sitting at a corner table, drooling and snorting and taking occasional talon swipes at sixth-graders who stray too close.

Cyril says, "Now watch."

Slowly, casually, Cat strolls up to Wilson's table. He gives her a nasty look, but she leans close to him and whispers something. His eyes glow green with bloodlust, but he gives her a skeptical sideways look. Cat shrugs and walks away.

"I don't get it," says Jake.

"Just watch!" Cyril tells him, grinning.

As Cat crosses the lunch room, Wilson swivels almost violently and snarls something at his troops. They look

3. Heebie-jeebies are small bacteria that implant themselves on your skin. These bacteria literally make your skin "crawl." After getting the heebie-jeebies once, my face actually crawled down my shoulder and ended up on the palm of my hand. It was disturbing until I realized that I could hold my hand up over walls and spy on people.

confused. Then he yells at them and jumps to his feet. They all leap up too.

Leaving all their stuff on the table, the Wolf Pack roars out of the lunchroom in a wild rush.

A few seconds pass.

Then Cat returns to their table. She turns and makes eye contact with Cyril. She nods.

Cyril nods back.

"She's good," says Jake admiringly. "She's very, very good."

"But they'll be back soon," says Lucas.

Lexi leaps to her feet. "I'll post sentry at the north door," she says.

Lucas takes off running. "I've got the south door," he shouts.

Jake shakes his head in awe.

"What a team!" he says.

Across the room, Cat nimbly rifles through Wilson's book bag but doesn't find what she wants. She starts shuffling through papers and books left on the tabletop. After a few tense seconds, she plucks up a small yellow slip of paper. She reads it, then turns toward Cyril again and nods dramatically.

Slipping the yellow note into her pocket, she slinks away, cool as a frozen cucumber.

Cyril and Jake leap to their feet, applauding.

"Bravo!" calls Jake. "Bravo!"

"What donkeys." Cyril laughs. "Leaving their stuff unguarded, right out in the open! Ha!"

The boys rush across the lunchroom toward Cat, who now waves the yellow note at them from the south exit door, next to Lucas. As Jake and Cyril hurry away, Lavina the Lunch Lady lumbers over and starts wiping down their lunch table. When she reaches Lucas's lunch and book bag, she glances around quickly. This corner of the room is now deserted.

Over by the south door, Team Spy Gear exchanges high fives with one another and Cat.

Meanwhile, with remarkably deft fingers, Lavina picks up the Spy Gear casebook.

She slips it into her apron pocket.

Then Lavina wheels her wastebasket slowly across the room and exits into the school kitchen.

6

GARBAGE TIME

After bidding Cat good-bye and thanks with a manly handshake, Cyril rejoins Team Spy Gear at the lunch table. Everyone gathers around the yellow note.

It reads:

TANGO SIERRA!
WPM 1208 0700 LNE

Lexi frowns and says, "Why would Brill want to meet so early on a Saturday? That's nuts! And if it's so hush-hush, why gather at their usual place?"

The others just stare at the note.

After a moment, Lucas says, "Uh, where does it say *any* of that in this note?"

Lexi looks confused. She points at the note. "Right there," she says.

Cyril nods. "Well, now that I think of it, Tango Sierra is military code for the letters *T* and *S*, which often means 'top secret.'"

Jake nods too, staring at the note. "Ah, I get it now," he says.

Lucas grimaces. "Share with us, will you?"

Jake grins and runs his finger over the note's message as he deciphers it: "*WPM* means Wolf Pack meeting. 1208 is actually twelve dash zero-eight, or December Eighth— which is this Saturday. 0700 is 'oh-seven hundred hours' or seven o'clock in the morning. And *LNE* no doubt stands for Loch Ness Elementary, the Pack's usual prowl." He looks over at Lexi. "Girl, you've got some serious parallel processing going on in that brain of yours."

Lexi looks confused again. She says, "All I did was read the note."

Jake laughs. "Okay, so anyway," he says, "this looks like a Pack meeting we should infiltrate." He turns to Cyril. "I don't think we could ask Cat to go deep cover on this one, do you?"

Cyril shakes his head no. "Pack meetings are members only, I hear," he says. "No girls allowed."

"Pigs," says Lexi darkly.

"Their loss and our gain," says Jake. "Lucas, let's log this note in the casebook and work up a plan."

"Roger," says Lucas. He looks around the table. "Uh, where's the casebook? Didn't I leave it out?" He opens his book bag and starts digging around. "Hmmm, not in here. Hey guys, who picked it up?"

The others make gestures that indicate no knowledge of such an action.

Now Lucas looks sick. "Crap!" he says. He looks around the room. "Who took it?"

Jake examines the tabletop. "Say, doesn't this lunch table look a lot *cleaner* than when we left it a minute ago?"

He turns to look at Cyril. Their eyes widen at the same time.

"The Lunch Lady!" they say in unison.

"Oh, no!"

"Quick!"

The team quickly gathers stuff and hurries across the debris-strewn lunchroom. Lunch is almost over, and the place resembles the aftermath of a windstorm. As Jake leads the team into the kitchen area, he notices his brother's gloomy face. He reaches over and grabs Lucas's shoulder.

"Head up, dog," he says. "We'll find it. It's all good."

Lucas gives a dismal nod.

In the kitchen, Jake spins a quick story to the lunch supervisor about a lost algebra notebook. He learns that all lunch trash goes directly into the Dumpsters behind the school.

The kids hurry out the back kitchen door onto a small loading dock.

"The Dumpsters are over there!" says Lexi, pointing.

"Excellent!"

"Let's go!"

"Yes!" says Cyril. "And let's hurry! I really can't *wait* to sift through rotten mounds of marinated filth."

Two foul-smelling, industrial-size metal Dumpsters lean against the back wall of the building. Jake approaches the nearest one and pushes up its heavy lid. Deep bass laughter rises from inside.

"Great," says Jake.

"Maybe you'd better toss in a concussion grenade first," says Cyril.

Suddenly, a putrid, black, vomitous mass spills out of the Dumpster. Its greasy skin sprouts wriggling feelers and antennae.

"Aaaaaaghhh!" shouts Cyril.

He tries to run but the moldy, decomposing stink-beast seizes him. Slimy creeper-tendrils start snaking up Cyril's nostrils and down his throat and yes, we've gone too far with this dark, horrific fantasy, so let's just open our eyes again and report what's *really* happening, shall we?

Actually, the Rancid Stench Entity merely pools and spreads around their ankles.

Now Jake rises up on his toes and peeks into the

Dumpster. The author cannot describe what Jake sees inside, not without yorking all over his keyboard, so let's just say that the sight of school-lunch waste is not something you want to see, ever, unless you want to be haunted by gruesome Septic Food-Worm nightmares for the rest of your life.

Jake, turning green, tries to keep a stiff upper lip.

He says, "Okay, okay, I'll, I'll, like, I'll crawl in first." He stares into the Dumpster. "But somebody hold my ankles." He suppresses a sick belch. "If I yell or shriek, pull me out, like, really fast and stuff."

"Right," says Cyril, peeking into the Dumpster too. "Wow. Don't touch that glowing stuff, okay? You know, just in case it's radioactive or possibly antimatter positrons." Cyril nods at Jake and smiles big. Then he starts backing away from the Dumpster. He adds, "Either way, you're a dead man."

"Thank you, Mr. Science," says Jake grimly.

Lexi suddenly points to the other end of the loading dock.

"Hey!" she calls. "Isn't that the Lunch Lady's wastebasket cart?"

"Where?" asks Lucas.

"There, behind those boxes," says Lexi.

Sure enough, Lavina's cart sits behind a stack of empty food shipping crates.

"I think it is!" says Lucas excitedly.

As Luke and Lexi rush to the cart, Jake backs away from the Dumpster, which emits a disappointed, hungry sigh. Jake belches again and says, "I won't eat again for weeks."

Cyril nods at the Dumpster. "Neither will he," he says.

"Woo-hoo!" shouts Lucas across the dock. "Here it is! Right on top!"

He waves the Spy Gear casebook at Jake and Cyril.

"Awesome," says Jake. "The Lunch Lady must have scooped it into her cart by accident."

As Team Spy Gear examines the casebook, the bell rings, ending lunch period. The four make hurried arrangements to meet after school at Cyril's house. Everyone agrees that Friday would be the best day for their expedition into the Old North Stand, to avoid homework conflicts and allow extra time if the trek runs late. Then each kid scurries off to his/her next class.

Nobody notices the bulbous yellow eyeball glaring at them through a crack in the cafeteria staff room door.

Behind a green Mercury minivan in the Carrolton Mall parking lot, Marco scoops his dreadlocks into a tight bunch at the back of his head. He pulls a hairnet over the wild hair.

Then he peers very, very carefully around the green vehicle.

This van is parked just yards from the Food Court

entrance. Two huge uniformed guards keep watch near the doorway. Both wear impenetrable sunglasses. Both sport nasty-looking sidearm pistols in high holsters. Nearby, their white Mall Security car idles at the curb.

Marco barely breathes.

This is not my gig, he thinks.

Suddenly, he hears the rumbling roar of a big engine to his right. He turns to see a mall shuttle bus pull up next to the white security car, cutting off his view. Marco thinks for a second, then quickly slinks out from behind the van and approaches the shuttle bus.

Marco assumes the shuttle bus will wait at least a minute or two before moving off. When he reaches it, he looks both ways—coast is clear, no cars—and then drops to the ground. Rolling onto his back, he scoots under the bus.

"I belong at a keyboard," mutters Marco to himself. "In a dark room."

Shuffling completely under the bus, he emerges near the rear quarter panel of the Mall Security car. The bus is very close to the car, so the gap between is small. Still on his back, Marco scoots just under the car's fender and reaches into his pocket.

He pulls out an Agent Tracker bug unit.

He turns it on.

Then he hooks it carefully under the rim of the car's fender and scoots back under the bus.

As he does this, the shuttle bus engine roars again. Marco, wild-eyed, scrambles and kicks hard. He emerges from under the bus just as it starts to move. With a graceless dive, he skids into hiding behind the green minivan as the bus pulls away.

Panting and cursing to himself, Marco peeks carefully around the van again.

Now the balding man in the blue lab coat, Dr. Hork, bursts from the mall entrance carrying a lunch sack. Looking unhappy, he staggers toward the Mall Security car. The two burly guards immediately fall in beside him, scanning the area as they walk. They strike Marco as being efficient, deadly professionals.

Especially that one with the shaved head.

A SHOCKING DISCOVERY

3:09 p.m. Friday, December 7.

Cyril mans his familiar post at HQ, preparing to monitor field operations from the main console in the Stoneship Toys warehouse control room, known by its code designation, Hotel Quebec. He runs through a mental checklist, swiveling to check the live video feeds from the field Minicams.

Then Cyril leans to the console microphone.

"Testing on Spy Link open channel," he says in a businesslike monotone. "Go Team North, all units report, over."

Roger, Hotel Quebec, echoes Jake's voice from the console speakers. **One here, over.**

"Roger that," says Cyril.

This is Go Team North, Unit Two, calls Lucas. **Do you read, over?**

"Got you marked, Two," says Cyril, adjusting the volume knob.

There is a long pause.

Finally, Cyril says, "Unit Three, do you copy, over?" Pause. "Go Team North, Unit Three? Are you there, over?"

I, uh, really have to go to the bathroom, says Lexi over the speakers.

Cyril grins. "Ah, Unit Three, Hotel Quebec here, you are cleared to go," he says. "Repeat, all systems are go for that maneuver, over?"

He hears Bixby's laughter in the speakers.

Hey, kid, try those bushes over there, says Jake.

Yeah, says Lucas. We'll move ahead and give you privacy.

Cyril, you can't see me, can you? asks Lexi, sounding uncomfortable.

Now, if you know the Stoneship situation, you know this isn't just a crazy paranoid question. Whoever built the amazing surveillance and communications center in the warehouse also planted dozens and dozens of video Mini-cams throughout the surrounding forest. Clearly, somebody wanted to keep a close eye on activity in Stoneship Woods. But why? To watch for intruders? Or was something going on in the woods—something sinister that must be monitored closely? These are excellent questions by the author, and you can bet they'll be in the Study Guide in the back of the book, so I hope you're taking good notes.

Cyril clicks the console mouse to open a viewing window with thumbnails of all available live camera feeds. "No, no, no, nope, no," he murmurs as he scans the display. "Nothing. No sign of you, Unit Three."

Whew! sighs Lexi.

Hey, here it is, says Jake. This is the Old North Stand boundary fence.

Wow! says Lucas. It's a beast!

Listen, says Jake. Do you hear that?

Yeah, Lucas answers. And look over there.

There is a brief silence. Then Cyril hears the concern in Jake's voice as he reports: Hotel Quebec, we've got a problem here, over.

Lucas stares up at a pair of yellow signs hanging on a huge, humming, wire-and-metal fence.

Danger: Restricted Area
No Trespassing

Next to that, another sign:

Warning: Electric Fence
10,000 Volts
Jutland Security Ltd
Pulse Induction Perimeter Fencing

Underneath this is a simple drawing of a human hand touching a line with jagged bolts of electricity shooting out.

"We got us a hot fence here, man," says Jake.

How bad is it? asks Cyril via Spy Link.

"Bad," says Jake.

Is it those polytape strips that keep out deer and whatever? asks Cyril. Just smash through with a big branch or something.

"No, dude, this is a heavy-duty security fence," says Lucas. "It's *huge*, at least twelve feet high, and the power hum is audible. According to the sign here, the output is ten thousand volts."

Wow, says Cyril, impressed.

"Yeah, this is no wildlife barrier," agrees Jake. He shakes his head. "It's meant to keep *people* out. You only see this kind of thing used around prisons or military installations, or maybe for border control."

Lexi pushes through some low saplings, buttoning her jacket. "It's getting colder," she says. Then she sees the electric fence and says, "Whoa!"

"Hot stuff," says Lucas.

She examines the two signs. "Did rangers do this?" she asks.

"Wow, good point," says Jake. "Nothing on either sign says that this is a government-installed fence." He frowns and adds, "Do you think this might be *private* land?"

"Maybe all the rumors that this is a federal habitat preserve aren't true," says Lucas.

A smokescreen, maybe, says Cyril.

Lexi starts walking along the fence line. She pushes through a scraggly, sun-starved evergreen bush and says, "Wow. Look here."

The Bixbys follow her. Through the bush, a small clearing opens up.

"Holy blinking toads!" exclaims Lucas, looking through the fence.

"Pure awesomeness!" says Jake.

Massive oak trunks, several feet thick, rise like great Roman columns just on the other side of the fence. The three kids lean back to look higher. No doubt these royal oaks rise hundreds of feet into the sky, but thick crisscrossing branches block sight of anything above fifty feet or so.

"And look there," says Lexi, pointing at another sign a few yards down the fence line.

It reads PRIVATE PROPERTY!

"Now that I think of it, I guess that makes more sense," says Jake. "If this was government-owned land, I doubt Viper could build a secret lab in here, right under the nose of the feds."

Lucas gets a sudden chill. He looks around. Then he says, "You know, anybody who deploys a ten-thousand-volt anti-intrusion system probably has a few *backup* security measures too." He peers up into the crosshatch of bare oak branches above and beyond the fence. "And I'll bet they're equally unpleasant."

"You mean, like, booby traps and stuff?" asks Lexi.

"Maybe," says Lucas.

Jake looks from Lucas to Lexi. He says, "Should we cancel this operation?"

"*What?*" gasps Lucas, horrified.

"No way!" shouts Lexi.

Jake smiles. "Okay, okay," he says.

Lucas and Lexi look relieved.

"Hotel Quebec," says Jake. "We need some quick online research."

I'm your Google Man, Cyril says. Just give me a topic, dude.

Jake turns and pushes back through the evergreen bush, then reexamines the fence warning sign. "What can you tell us about the pulse induction perimeter fencing manufactured by a company called Jutland Security? We need a way to shut down or bypass a twelve-foot electric fence."

Roger that, Unit One, says Cyril in his best Mission Control voice. Online search . . . commencing . . . now.

Lucas approaches the fence. "Whatever Cyril finds," he says, "it will involve at least one of us getting to the other side of this fence." He turns to face Lexi. "Of this I have no doubt."

Lexi smiles so big her teeth nearly fall out.

Lugging his backpack, Marco tramps underneath the expressway, a long stretch of freeway overpass that spans the length of Carrolton from north to south. Above, cars and trucks buzz past in a steady torrent that sounds like a waterfall.

Down here, however, just a few cars motor past on County Road 44. The nose of a black BMW is just visible behind one of the huge support struts holding up the expressway.

Marco stops and looks around.

Near the strut, Marco notices a bush jiggling. He faces it and raises his hand.

The bush stops jiggling.

Marco frowns. He takes a few steps toward the bush.

"Hello?" he calls.

Suddenly, the bush starts shaking wildly as Marco hears what sounds like a falling body. He steps forward to see a pair of black-clad legs sticking out of the bush and kicking.

Marco rolls his eyes.

"Need a hand there, pal?" he asks.

Lexi gazes down at an eight-foot gap between the branch she stands on and another branch in the next tree. The far branch juts over the humming Jutland fence. Lexi is a gymnast. She's got mad skills. But even for Lexi, this is a bit much.

"Not good," she calls.

On the ground fifteen feet below her, Jake and Lucas exchange a look. If Lexi Lopez says some physical feat of derring-do is not good, then guess what? It's not good.

"Somebody cleared trees along the fence," calls Jake. "See those stumps?"

Lucas notes several rotting stumps on either side of the fence line. "Very thorough," he says.

Jake nods. "Somebody worked very hard to keep people out of the Old North Stand."

Suddenly he hears a loud cracking sound above. Both Bixbys look up to see Lexi dangle from the branch on the other side of the fence. But the branch is splintering! Hanging on tight, Lexi rides it downward—then drops lightly to the ground.

"I did it!" she shouts. *"Ha!"*

Lucas peers at her through the fence. "But how will you get back?" he asks.

Lexi looks stunned by this question.

"Are you kidding?" she says. "Cyril will figure out how I can turn off the fence. Right?"

Jake and Lucas just look at each other.

Back at Stoneship HQ, Cyril sorts a few pages of scribbled notes and flicks open the Spy Link channel. "This is Hotel Quebec, calling Go Team North, do you read me, over?" he says.

Go ahead, Hotel Quebec, answers Jake.

"All right, well, this is going to sound kind of grim, but bear with me, okay?" says Cyril.

Great, says Jake.

"First of all, and pay close attention here, be aware that the fence can kill you," says Cyril, looking at his notes. "Don't touch the fence. Don't breathe on the fence. Don't even *think* about the fence."

Roger that, says Jake.

"Now listen carefully," says Cyril. "An electric fence surrounding twenty acres of land is a pretty long fence. It has to be divided into twenty or thirty electrified zones. Electricity flowing to all of these zones runs through a central power controller, located most likely in a very secure, hidden, and heavily guarded location." He draws a big black X through the page. "So forget that."

Cyril flips to another page.

"Now, each individual fence zone has its own *local* power box, with a keypad. If you actually find this box, you can disarm the electrified zone if you enter the keypad code. Amazingly enough, we don't have any keypad codes. So forget that, too."

Hey, this is going great so far, says Lucas.

"Yes, well, it gets greater," says Cyril. "It *is* possible to simply cut the power lines running into or out of a local power box, thus neutralizing that zone. But in any Jutland perimeter fencing system, if you cut power lines you trigger a Zone Intrusion alert. This activates a loud siren, searchlights, and a three-hundred-sixty-degree rotating security camera." He pauses. "No doubt this also triggers the release of the winged monkeys."

So forget that, says Jake.

"Yes, forget that," agrees Cyril.

He flips to one last page of his notes.

"Guys, Jutland Security makes a very nasty fence," he says. "I'm afraid your only bet is to propel yourselves *completely over* the fence without touching anything. I suggest using standard pole-vaulting techniques." Cyril grins and leans way back in the leather captain's chair, clasping his hands behind his head. "Or, ha-ha, you could build a catapult from native logs and vines, jump aboard, and fire away!"

"Very funny," says a deep voice right behind Cyril, and the HQ lights go out.

Cyril starts so violently that his chair tips over backward. When it hits the ground, he finds himself staring straight up into a dark face.

"Hey, dude," says Cyril.

"You should be more vigilant," says Marco.

"I was busy."

"Not a good excuse."

Cyril tries to rise out of the fallen chair, but Marco gently pushes him back down. Cyril frowns.

"I've got someone who wants to meet you," says Marco, keeping his hand on Cyril's chest.

"Is it a fan?" asks Cyril.

"Yes. A *big* fan."

"Okay, but no autographs."

Marco reaches into his pocket and pulls out a small black scarf.

He says, "First, however, he insists I do this."

He blindfolds Cyril.

THE BIG EMPTY

And so our three intrepid explorers walk along a humming electric fence—two Bixbys on the outside, one monkey-girl on the inside. They look for two more trees close enough together to create a bridge of branches over the electrified barrier.

So far, no luck. But Lexi feels lucky, nonetheless. Very, very lucky.

"These trees are *humongous*," says Lexi happily, staring up the trunk of a massive red oak. "Dude, I could get lost up there for, like, days." Lexi loves trees, having spent at least half her life in them so far.

"They are wicked big," agrees Lucas.

Jake peers up into the canopy of another ancient oak. He can almost feel its age and wisdom. Something about these great trees calms him, despite the possible danger lurking within the stand.

As they round a bend in the fence line, Lexi suddenly stops and says, "Whoa."

Just ahead, an entrance gate in the fence spans a narrow, rutted dirt road, wide enough for one car. Lucas looks around warily. He says, "An entry point like this probably has security surveillance." He turns to Jake and asks, "So what's the plan?"

Jake thinks a second.

He glances through the fence at Lexi, who walks over to a muscular-looking oak and places a worshipful palm on its trunk. He thinks, *Okay, she's happy, but she's also trapped.*

Then he gives Lucas a significant look. Speaking calmly, he says, "I think it's worth the risk to check out the gate."

Lucas glances at Lexi and nods. "Okay," he says. "But let's get our story straight."

"What do you mean?"

"You know, in case we get caught. Like, what exactly are we doing here?"

Jake grins. "Standard fallback position," he says. He scrunches up his voice. "Hey, we're just a bunch of stupid little kids, lost in the woods."

"But will Viper's thugs buy that?" asks Lucas. "Don't you think they *know* us by now?"

Jake lowers his voice so Lexi can't hear. "Maybe. Maybe not. It doesn't matter."

Lucas nods. "Okay."

Jake glances over at Lexi again. Then he looks back down the fence line. The two trees she used to cross over are the only ones within thirty feet of either side of the fence.

"Okay, let's do it," he says.

Jake marches directly to the gate. Lucas follows.

Lexi moves parallel to them on the other side. "What? Do what?" She looks up at the gate. "What are we going to do?"

Lucas examines the gate mechanisms. The gate itself is an automatic side-rolling unit; several V-groove wheels are attached along the gate's bottom frame. These wheel grooves rest on a raised steel track, so the gate can roll open and shut. On either side of the gate, solid steel podiums rise from the ground, with keypads for code entry. Fixed atop two of the gate posts are red beacon lamps.

"Very sophisticated," says Lucas, shaking his head.

Jake looks up at the beacon lamps. "I don't see any cameras," he says.

"Oh, they're watching us," says Lucas. "Trust me."

"How do you know that?" asks Lexi.

Suddenly, the gate buzzes loudly.

Startled, the Bixbys back away as the beacon lamps

start flashing. Then the gate starts rolling slowly sideways. As it rolls, the red beacons keep flashing, emitting a loud buzz with each flash. This continues until the gate finally slides completely open. Then the flashing stops. After a few more clicks, all sound stops too.

The three kids exchange looks.

"Gee, how nice of them," says Lucas nervously.

"The question is," Jake whispers to Lucas, "are they letting Lexi *out* or letting us *in?*"

They look at the gate, which offers nothing in the way of answers.

It remains open, motionless, and silent.

Cyril sits blindfolded in the Stoneship HQ captain's chair. The lights are still out. It's really dark. *What's going on?* Nobody knows. It's too dark. Cyril's eyes are the camera in this scene. So unfortunately, we're in bad shape, sightwise. I should also mention that "darkness" is the key word here.

Feeling vulnerable, Cyril folds his arms across his chest. Then a big hand settles on his shoulder. Cyril jumps and screams.

"Be cool, hair boy," says Marco, near Cyril's ear.

"I can't," says Cyril. "Because gosh, I'm just having *too much fun.*"

"I got your back," whispers Marco. "Don't worry."

Cyril nods. This simple statement calms him a bit.

"Lights!" calls Marco to someone.

Around the edges of the blindfold, Cyril detects the glow of light again. Then he hears a distant scuffling sound and a grunt of effort. Someone is climbing the recessed rungs from the warehouse floor to the control room.

Suddenly, voices squawk from the console speakers. Hotel Quebec, Hotel Quebec, calls Jake. We have a situation here. Over?

Cyril turns his head toward the console.

"Can I answer him?" he asks.

"No," says Marco.

"Why not?"

Hotel Quebec, says Jake urgently. Do you read me?

"Hey, Jake needs me," says Cyril.

Requesting overhead scan, says Jake on the speakers. Cyril, please advise. Our current location—

With a click, the voice ends.

"What are you doing?" says Cyril, getting agitated. "Who shut down the Spy Link?"

"Your friends are in no danger," says a deep, raspy voice—an inhuman voice that sounds slightly robotic. "None whatsoever."

Cyril sits up straight. "Wow," he says. "Is there a Corellian cyborg in the room?"

"I'm altering my voice with a warp," says the scary voice. "A digital LP filter mask, to be precise."

"Why?" asks Cyril.

"I don't want you to recognize my voice, should we meet again."

Cyril snorts. "Why would I care?"

"Because, well," begins the voice. "Because I'll be, I'm very, look, never mind." Cyril hears the rasp of heavy, annoyed breathing. "We have our reasons."

"Oh, *do* we?" snaps Cyril. "Hey, Darth, how do you know my friends are safe?"

Cyril feels Marco's fingers tap him lightly on the shoulder. "Dude, trust him."

"Why?" says Cyril, turning his head up toward Marco's voice.

"Because you have no choice!" rasps the deep voice with growing irritation.

"Hmmm," says Cyril. "Okay." He turns his head from Marco back toward the deep voice. "So, like, you guys *know* each other?"

"Of course we do!" says the voice.

Marco taps Cyril's shoulder again. "He's Agency," says Marco. "Interrogated me after my Internet caper in Viper's employ." He takes a deep breath. "He's the reason I'm not rotting in some Middle Eastern prison right now. So I owe him a few favors."

Cyril nods. "Got it," he says quietly.

"Please listen carefully," says the voice. "Much is at stake."

Cyril hears footsteps and the swishing movement of a heavy coat. Then a loud metallic clatter. Then a muffled, angry gasp. Then someone scuffling around on the floor near Cyril's feet.

A few seconds later, Marco says, "Say, can I give you a hand with those?"

"No!" says the robotic voice.

Another pause, then Marco says, "I think one rolled under the desk over there."

"I see it!" says the angry voice, rising in front of Cyril.

Even through the blindfold, Cyril can sense a huge dark presence looming in front of him. He hears a familiar rattling sound—yes, the rattle of dice.

"Hold out your hand," commands the warped voice.

Cyril does so, and a pair of dice drops into his palm. He closes his hand around them. "Did you want to play Yahtzee?" asks Cyril. "Because it won't be fair, really. This blindfold gives you a pretty big advantage."

"Actually, you could just feel the indentations on the dice," says Marco.

"That's a good point," says Cyril.

"It would be tedious, but—"

Cyril runs his fingers over the dice. "Yes, yes," he says, "that's a two. That's a six. You're absolutely right."

"*We're not playing Yahtzee!*" howls the dark voice, quite loudly. "Listen to me, funny boy. I left these dice for you, not long ago."

"You mean the snake eyes?" asks Cyril. "The painfully obvious hint about Viper?"

"You seem to be so very good with ciphers," says the voice, with a dark, menacing edge. "Before I ask you more about such things, let me make something perfectly clear. You should know that—" Another loud clatter rattles the room. "Leave it!" howls the voice.

"Right," says Marco. "We'll just, you know, tidy up later."

Now Cyril hears the raspy, warped breathing just inches from his face. "Listen and listen good," says the voice with unbridled anger now. "Viper is no joke. Viper is no laughing matter. Viper is ruthless, brilliant, and quite vicious about eliminating obstacles that annoy him. Do you understand me now, funny boy?" he hisses right in Cyril's face.

"No," says Cyril, trying not to smile. "Could you repeat that again? I wasn't listening."

Jake yanks his Spy Link headset out of his ear and looks at it. "Maybe mine's not working," he says. He nods at Lucas and adds, "Try yours."

"Hotel Quebec, do you read me?" says Lucas. "Are you there, Charlie Whiskey, over?"

No reply.

Lucas sighs. "This seems to happen a lot with Cyril," he says.

As Jake slides his headset back over his ear, Lexi walks through the open gate and joins the boys. She taps her own Spy Link headset and says, "Maybe he's checking something on another channel."

Lucas snorts. "Right," he says.

Jake looks at him. "He probably just punched the wrong button again."

"Whatever."

Jake says, "Well, Lexi's out, anyway."

They stand and watch the gate for a while. Nothing happens. Then, abruptly, Jake walks through. Lucas and Lexi exchange a look and follow him. Now all three kids stand inside the fenced enclosure of the Old North Stand, staring back at the gate.

"Well, it's still open," says Lexi.

"But for how long?" says Lucas.

"Let's try something," says Jake. "Come on."

He starts walking away from the gate, down the rutted road. Lexi and Lucas shrug at each other, then follow him. Just as they enter the canopy of taller oak trees, the gate buzzes loudly. With beacons flashing red again, it begins to close.

"Come on!" yells Jake.

They burst into a wild sprint, trying to beat the slowly closing gate. But as they get closer, the gate emits another long buzz, then reverses direction. It rolls back open again!

Jake skids to a stop. "Interesting," he says.

"Yes," says Lucas. "Very."

"Will it open like that whenever we walk up to it?" wonders Lexi.

Both of the younger children look up at Jake. He pulls his baseball cap lower on his forehead. Then he grins. And folks, this is one of his *better* grins.

Listen: Jake Bixby is careful about most things in life. He's deliberate. He likes to think things through. But for some reason, whenever Jake finds himself in certain situations—like this one, for example—something in his gut pulls him in a direction. Then he just follows the pull. All of his "thinking" happens instantly, in a quantum second.

"Let's go," he says.

He turns his back to the open gate and follows the road into the big trees.

Smiling, Lucas and Lexi follow.

The rutted road ends at a small asphalt parking lot, empty now but neatly marked with slots for twenty cars.

"Stoats alive!" says Lucas. "This must be where the secret lab workers park."

"Maybe," says Jake. "But where's the lab?" He looks around the small clearing. "I don't see any buildings, do you?"

"But it's not twelve o'clock!" says Lucas excitedly. "Remember, the Omega clue said something about looking at twelve o'clock." His eyes grow saucer-wide. "Maybe at twelve o'clock, the lab rises up out of the ground or something!"

Jake just gazes at Lucas for a moment. Then he says, "Yeah, and then it goes *Boo!*"

"Hey, I'm just throwing out ideas."

Jake grins. "I know," he says.

Lexi frowns. "But that sounds crazy," she says.

"It *is* crazy!" says Lucas excitedly, bouncing on his toes. As you can probably tell, Lucas loves this part of spy work—the part where you concoct outrageous theories that *just might be true*, but probably aren't.

"Maybe this is where the spaceship lands," says Lexi.

Jake looks up. The crowns of the surrounding big trees are so broad that no sky is visible. "Doesn't look like it could," he says.

"Yeah." Lucas nods. "I think this whole stand is pretty much covered in canopy."

"Hey, what's that?" says Jake, pointing across the parking lot.

He leads the team to a small clearing on the far side of the lot. A split-rail fence surrounds the area, but an open wooden gate leads to a well-groomed trail that disappears into the big trees. A trail marker reads CHAMPION LOOP, 0.7 MILES. In the center of the clearing, a large plaque with a colorful schematic drawing is mounted on a podium. Under the plaque is a small Plexiglas box.

The trio approaches the plaque. It reads:

The Harvey P. Wilks Arboretum
A Private Old-Growth Preserve

"A private arboretum?" says Jake, surprised.

"What's an arboretum?" asks Lexi.

"It's sort of like a special tree garden," says Lucas. "Where trees and shrubs are protected and preserved for study."

"Sweet!" says Lexi. "I totally want one of those when I grow up."

Jake points at the schematic drawing. "That's an area map," he says.

Lucas adds, "Yes, a *trail* map."

Indeed, the entire Old North Stand appears to be an arboretum accessible via trail. The main route, Champion Loop, runs (as its name suggests) in a large loop around the outer perimeter of the stand. Several other trails with names like Red Oak Run, Maple Twin, and Founders Grove crisscross through the middle of the map.

The small box under the plaque is labeled VISITORS' GUIDE. Jake opens the lid and pulls out a brochure. It opens to reveal a printed version of the same map that's on the plaque.

"Looks like some of the trees are named too," says Jake, pointing at red spots on the map. "Big Redhead. Mother Nature. Old Baldy."

"What are we waiting for?" says Lucas. "Let's hike, dudes!"

The three set off down the main trail. The crisp December air is bracing, and the smell of the pristine forest is cool and clean. Many of the trees are crazy huge— trunks twenty feet around, with twisting, ropy roots and the lowest branches fifty feet up. Placards name them and give vital statistics—species, height, circumference, and so on.

"Hard to believe this area is actually part of Stoneship Woods," says Jake, gazing upward as he walks. "It's, like, beautiful."

"I don't feel scared at all," says Lucas. "I like it here."

"Dude, I want to *live* here," says Lexi, eyeing the massive trunk of a hoary old oak named Quirky Ned. The placard at its base describes it as a "National Champion Northern Red Oak" with a height of 141 feet and a girth of 18 feet. She looks up into its canopy. "You can't even see *halfway* up. Look at all those branches!"

Lucas looks up too. "Yep, that's a paradise for monkey-girls up there," he says.

The team hikes for an hour, first completing the full Champion Loop, and then winding through the interior trails, all of which are neatly maintained. Jake points out that even the autumn's fallen leaves appear to have been carefully raked from the walking paths. More important, the team finds absolutely no sign of a lab. In fact, there's no sign of any manmade structure whatsoever. Just trees—lots of trees.

Suddenly, the three hear static in their Spy Link earphones. Then: **Go Team North, do you read me, over?** calls Cyril.

Jake brightens. "Hey, man, where you been?" he asks. "We've been calling you for an hour."

Cyril says, **Long story. Very long. I'll fill you in later. More important, where are you? What's up?**

Jake gives Cyril a quick rundown of the past hour. "And not a sign of a lab or even a secret entrance to a lab." Jake gazes upward. "And dude, these trees are *really* tall. They're awesome."

"Cyril, we considered a possible underground facility, along the lines of Firelight Studios," adds Lucas. "But we've seen absolutely no sign of the necessary ventilation or power system—no pipes, no boxes, nothing in the ground. We can't even find a power source for the electric fence."

Hmmm, says Cyril, lowering his voice. **That analysis certainly jibes with what my sources are telling me.**

Jake raises a brow in amusement. "Sources?" he says. "What sources?"

There's a long pause. Then: **Guys, I suggest you call it a day,** says Cyril. **You're not going to find anything.**

The three field team members exchange puzzled looks. Then Jake says, "Cyril, how do you know this?"

It's a long story.

"Right. Can we get a summary?"

There is another long pause. The field team hears muffled talking, as if a hand is clamped over the mike. Then Cyril comes back and says, **Just get back to Hotel Quebec. I'll explain once you get here.**

"Just to be perfectly clear," says Jake slowly, "you're saying we should leave the arboretum now, because we won't find any lab here?"

Correct.

"And you know this from trusted sources," says Jake. "But you can't discuss them."

Not over an open channel, says Cyril. **If you catch my drift.**

Lucas says, "Cyril, are you suggesting that some unauthorized outside party is monitoring our Spy Link channel?"

I might be suggesting that, yes.

Jake turns to Lucas, who shrugs, and then to Lexi, who looks disappointed.

"Okay," says Jake. "We're coming in."

Excellent command decision, Jake, says Cyril. **I'm proud to be your teammate.** He raises his voice. **You hear that out there? Proud!**

Jake grins. "Whatever," he says.

He pulls out his map and consults it briefly. Then he leads Lexi and Lucas down the Chisholm East trail, heading back to the trailhead.

"This is, like, my favorite place in the world," sighs Lexi as she trudges behind Jake.

Lucas pulls up beside her. He says, "You're sure the aircraft lights you saw were over this stand?"

"Positive."

"In the clouds, above these tall trees?" asks Lucas, gesturing around them.

"Yes."

Both of them stare upward into the impenetrable canopy above them. "Jake's right, it would be pretty hard for anything that big to drop through those branches," says Lucas. "Maybe it was just flying over, heading somewhere else."

"I guess," says Lexi, shrugging.

Ten minutes later they reach the main gate. As they approach, the mechanism buzzes, the beacon flashes, and the gate rolls open. As the trio trudges through, Jake glances up at the gate. He shakes his head.

"This makes *no* sense," he says, with a hint of frustration.

Cyril's voice crackles in his ear: How so?

"Dude, why would somebody go to the huge expense of erecting almost a mile of electrified security fence," says Jake, "but then add a wicked-hot gate that just, like, opens up whenever somebody walks up to it?" He looks over at his brother. "Does that make any sense to you?"

Lucas is about to answer when the distant roar of car engines drifts through the trees.

"Vehicles incoming!" says Jake. "Quick!"

Jake, Lexi, and Lucas dive into the thick bushes beside the rutted lane. After a few seconds, two long black sedans fishtail up the road. The lead car hits its brakes and skids to a halt just a few feet from the gate, and the second car stops behind the first. Peering carefully from the bushes, Jake can see dark-tinted windows that shield the car occupants from sight.

For a few seconds, the cars sit at the gate, engines rumbling . . . waiting.

"The gate's not opening!" whispers Lucas. He shakes his head. "It's not letting them in!" Then he points at the front license plate of the lead car.

Jake nods. "Government plates," he says.

"The feds!" hisses Lucas.

There are a few more seconds of tense inaction. Motors rev up loudly, but the cars do not move. Then, finally, the second car starts backing away slowly. The lead car follows suit, backing twenty, thirty feet.

Then the lead car guns its engine.

With its tires kicking up gravel, it barrels directly toward the gate. When it strikes, a loud explosive *pop!* rises above the screeching, rending, earsplitting sound of the car tearing through the chain-link barrier. A shower of sparks flies upward, then bounces on the car as it bulldozes through the gate. The gate's red beacon light tumbles and shatters on the car's roof.

"That vehicle is *seriously* armored," whispers Jake.

Lucas, mesmerized by the spectacle, has risen slightly from the bushes. Jake reaches up and yanks his brother back into cover. But as the second car follows the lead car up the lane, it suddenly stops, just ten feet from Team Spy Gear's hiding spot in the woods.

"Crud!" hisses Jake. "Get ready to run!"

The black car sits in the lane, unmoving.

9

DARK ENCOUNTERS

The second sedan sits ominously in the lane, snorting smoke from its front grille like a great black bull minus the horns and, well, minus any other feature that resembles a black bull, except it's black. And of course, cars don't actually snort smoke through their grilles. But then, neither do bulls. So perhaps the analogy is more apt than one might think, and hey, look, the second black sedan just drove through the gate.

Boy, that was a cheesy way to keep your attention, wasn't it?

As soon as the second sedan disappears down the lane, Jake, Lucas, and Lexi burst from the bushes and start running south.

"Two black cars, Cyril," pants Jake as he runs. "Government plates. They slammed right through the electric gate!"

Recommend radio silence, answers Cyril.

"What?"

Let's discuss it back here, folks.

Jake frowns but says, "Okay, roger that. We'll be in shortly."

It's only about a quarter of a mile to HQ, but the going is slow through the thick woods. Strangely, once the team leaves the old-growth arboretum behind, Stoneship Woods gets darker somehow, creepier, more oppressive— perhaps because the canopy is lower, or because the smaller trees keep whispering things like *Puny human sludge-bag!* as you run past, and then spit at you. Jake keeps feeling things on the back of his neck as he hops over tangled vines and ducks under grasping tree limbs.

The trio doesn't slow down until they reach the perimeter fence around the warehouse yard.

Up in the control room, Cyril sits in the captain's chair, drumming his fingers on the console. He's alone in the room. Marco's black scarf is wrapped stylishly around his neck. As Jake climbs up through the hatch, Cyril nods at him.

Jake nods back. "Nice scarf," he says.

Cyril whips it off his neck and looks at it. "Yes, it's very *dark*," he says.

"Did we miss anything?" asks Jake with a grin.

"Yes. You missed a party."

"So did you," says Jake. Now Lucas and Lexi follow him through the hatch.

"Well, my party was *partier*," says Cyril.

"Really?"

"Yes, it was." Cyril swivels his chair around to face everyone. "Witty conversation. Interesting people. Like Marco, for example."

Lexi looks around the room. "Where?"

"He left," says Cyril, examining his fingernails. "With the huge cyborg dude."

Jake frowns. "What?"

Cyril leans back in the chair and starts describing his blindfolded meeting with the Dark Man. "He didn't say a whole lot," says Cyril. "Mostly he just issued bleak warnings and threats and such." He shrugs. "You know, the usual."

"Marco brought him up here?" asks Jake, frowning.

"Yep."

"What exactly did he want?"

"Well, that's a good question," says Cyril. "At first, I figured he was just fishing desperately for information because he's such a doofus. I mean, the guy knocked over about twelve things in the hour he was here. But Marco claims he's legit." He gives Jake a look. "And he knows all about Viper."

Jake nods. "Interesting. So what's Viper up to? Did they discuss his overall plans?"

"No," says Cyril. "But they discussed Marco's theory about the quantum super-hacking thing for a freaking hour." He takes a deep breath. "It was a very *long* and *dark* hour, let me tell you."

"Wow," says Lucas. "A quantum computer. Could it really be true?"

"Yes, well, Darth Donkey seemed quite interested," says Cyril. "Marco explained it—ions and photons and frozen samples and blah blah blah. They decided a very large, expensive experimental lab would be needed for such a sophisticated project." He shrugs. "And then they both left. Didn't, even, say, *good-bye*." He puts a hand over his heart. "Cut me real deep."

Lucas says, "So you never saw the guy."

"Actually, I did," says Cyril. "I caught just a glimpse as they left. There." He points at a side monitor with a live feed of the south yard. "Dude was *huge*. Bigger than Marco, even. Dressed in black, head to toe. Hat, coat, shoes. I couldn't see his face, though." Cyril smirks. "He took a pretty good dive trying to get through the fence. Ouch!"

"So he told you about Viper," Lucas says.

"A little. Not much."

"And what did *you* tell *him*?" asks Lucas.

Cyril's eyes dart sideways. "About what?" he asks.

Lucas narrows his eyes and says, "About anything."

Cyril waves the scarf. "I told him about the Omega messages."

"You mean . . . the fragments?"

"Yeah," says Cyril nonchalantly.

"Why?" Lucas puts a hand to his forehead. "Why did you tell him?"

Cyril rolls his eyes in annoyance. "Look, he already *knew* about them, okay? Marco told him, apparently. So he wondered what they meant." He swivels his chair away from Lucas. "Why he cares about how a bunch of stupid little kids deciphered some stupid secret message is beyond me, Bixby."

"So you just forked over our top secret analysis of the messages?" says Lucas.

"Right. With a *big* honking fork."

Lucas glares at Cyril. "I'll bet he was thrilled to get such confidential Spy Gear stuff so *easily*."

Cyril glares back. "I wouldn't know!" he yells. "All I could see was a scarf!"

"Guys," says Jake. "Chill."

Both Cyril and Lucas huff out deep breaths. Lucas looks at Jake, then at Cyril.

"Okay, okay," says Lucas. "Sorry."

Cyril waves his hand. "Forget it," he says. "Actually, Robot Bob already knew about the Old North Stand. He said his people have searched the area and found nothing." Now Cyril stands up. "In fact, he says his people have been over every inch of Stoneship Woods in the past three months."

"His people?" says Jake. "*What* people?"

"I didn't ask."

"Why not?"

"Because I was on the verge of catatonic withdrawal from reality," says Cyril.

Jake notices that Cyril's knees are a little shaky. He gently pushes Cyril back into the chair. He says, "Dude, it must have been freakishly scary."

Cyril says, "Nah."

Jake grins. "I'd be barking insane right now."

"No, you wouldn't."

"Yes, I would."

Cyril sticks out a fist. Jake punches it.

"Anything else you can tell us?" asks Lucas.

"When Raspy Throat Man found out my Go Team was about to infiltrate the big trees, he grew super-agitated—which of course was fun for me," says Cyril. "Then he called in backup for you," says Cyril. "Seriously, that's what he called it: *backup*." He gives Jake a skeptical look.

"Really?" says Jake with interest.

"Yes," says Cyril. He lowers his voice to a mechanical growl and cups his hands over his mouth. "All units report to location Beta Tango with *all possible speed*."

"Hence the appearance of the black cars," says Lucas, nodding.

Lexi looks confused. "So wait—he's on *our* side?"

Cyril says, "Somehow, I think it's more complicated than that, kid."

Lucas nods. "Well, he's a G-man, apparently."

"What's a G-man?" asks Lexi.

"G for government. A federal agent."

"Oh, good," she says. "So the government will pay for poor Harvey's gate that they mashed to pieces."

"Sure," says Lucas. "The government always admits when it's wrong and then pays everybody back."

Cyril laughs loudly at this. Then he says, "Actually, you know, I just remembered an interesting tidbit. Twice, Scary Dark Man mentioned something he called 'the Agency.' First, he said that the Agency already checked the big tree area, I guess looking for a quantum computer lab too. The second mention was when he suggested that all secure communications, including the Omega Link *and* our Spy Link channels, might be compromised due to quantum hacking. He said, 'Viper has been a step ahead of the Agency for weeks now.'"

"So that's why he left us the dice clue and the 'no Omega' note," says Jake.

"Right," says Cyril.

"And that's why you wanted radio silence earlier," adds Jake.

"Right," says Cyril.

Jake's eyes darken. "Do you think Viper himself has sent us messages?"

"Very possibly," nods Cyril.

Lucas widens his eyes. "The Agency," he says. "Isn't that what the CIA calls itself?"

"I don't know," says Cyril. "I haven't worked there in years."

Lucas ignores Cyril. "Like, in movies and stuff," he says, getting excited. "CIA guys always call themselves the Agency. Like, you know, it's the *only* agency worthy of being called, you know, an *Agency*."

"I don't know," says Jake. He glances around. "Do you really think this place was a CIA spy post? I still find it hard to believe that the CIA, with its immense power and resources, would just abandon a post like this." He shakes his head. "That just doesn't make *sense*. I mean, why don't they just come back and take it over?"

"Because . . . they fear me," says Cyril. He jumps up into a karate stance.

Lucas grins and looks at the Omega Link, which sits on the corner of the console. "Yeah, you're right," he says to Jake. "I just thought it would be cool to get messages, like, from Langley headquarters." Then a thought hits him. "So whatever this Agency is, the Omega Link was originally connected to it. Maybe the Robot Voice Guy himself sent us messages."

"Maybe, but not the last batch," says Cyril. "Not the fragments. Remember, he didn't *know* about them. He learned about them from Marco. That was pretty clear from their conversation."

"Okay," says Jake, picking up the Omega Link. "So the latest Omega messages came from somewhere else."

"Like, say, from a mole," says a deep voice rising up through the floor hatch.

Everybody spins to face the hatch.

Marco pops up through the opening.

He waves. "Hello, children," he says.

The prospect of a mole working inside Viper's organization, sending messages via the Omega Link—wow! Plus Marco's direct contact with the Dark Man is amazingly exciting and scintillating and thrilling and all that. But it's getting dark.

That means it's time to get out of Stoneship Woods.

As Team Spy Gear jogs east down the access road through the darkening forest, they grill Marco about his encounters.

"He's been watching you from Day One," he says.

"You mean the Dark Man?" asks Lexi.

Marco nods. "Yeah, and that's a good name for him," he says. "The Dark Man."

"Marco, why would someone try to send a message about Viper's secret quantum computer lab to the Omega Link?" asks Jake.

"The mole is deep cover with the Agency," says

Marco. "Very, very deep. He hasn't surfaced to make contact in many, many months. As far as he knows, the Omega Link is still an Agency channel." Marco snorts. "He doesn't know he's actually messaging a bunch of middle-school kids instead."

Cyril, panting, looks over at Marco. "Hey, I got an A in Complex Math Impediments," he says.

Marco says, "So?"

"So don't underestimate me, Buster."

Lucas jogs up even with Marco. "Do you know who or what the Agency is?" he asks.

"No idea."

"CIA or NSA, maybe?"

"I really don't think so," says Marco. "This guy is on an entirely different level of covert spookiness." He looks at Jake. "Their operations are so black I don't think they even know who they are themselves."

"What's Dark Man look like?" asks Lexi.

"Can't say," says Marco as they approach the line of trees blocking passage onto County Road 44. "Dude keeps his collar high and hat low. And he always talks through that ridiculous voice filter."

Jake abruptly shushes everyone and holds up his hand.

"Let's check for wolves before we push through," he whispers.

"I don't believe that's necessary," says Cyril. "Remember, we have the Mall Sausage Butcher as escort."

"Right." Jake grins. "I forgot."

So the group pushes through the tree line and steps out onto the shoulder of County Road 44. No sign of the Wolf Pack.

Jake turns to Marco. "Where are you staying now?"

"I rent a converted garage behind a guy's house in the Old Town area east of the business district," says Marco. "Very shabby. Lots of bugs." He bobs his head, bouncing his dreadlocks. "I love it."

"Give us your phone number," says Jake.

"I can't afford a phone yet," says Marco with a rueful smile.

Lucas steps up to Marco. He says, "Then I'm about to bestow you with a great honor."

Marco turns his head suspiciously as Lucas slings his gadget backpack off his shoulder and opens it. He pulls out a Spy Link headset and base unit and hands them to Marco.

"Gosh, I'm speechless," says Marco blandly.

Lexi grins. "Then shut up, old man," she says.

Jake steps up to Marco and gives him a brotherly poke in the shoulder. Then he turns to the others. "Okay, before we all head home," he says. He points at Lucas. "Case summary to date."

Lucas clears his throat.

"Okay," he says. "Viper may have a working quantum computer, but it's not a *fully* working model, or else he'd already be Super King of the World, having hacked nuclear launch codes and raided international banks and stuff. But he's got a lab somewhere—we thought in the Old North Stand, but apparently not, since both the Agency and Team Spy Gear have gone over the area with a fine-tooth comb." He pauses.

"Is that all?" asks Jake, looking around.

"No," says Lexi.

"What else?"

She says, "Tomorrow morning we find out what the Wolf Pack is planning at Loch Ness."

"Excellent," says Jake.

Suddenly, a cell phone rings.

"That's mine," says Cyril. He whips his phone out of a pocket and flips it open to check the incoming number. Then he frowns. "I don't know this one." He looks around at the others.

"Go for it," says Jake.

Cyril presses the Answer button. "Hello?"

He listens for a second.

Then his eyes expand. "Oh, hey, Cat." He starts walking swiftly down County Road 44, heading south toward his house. "No, no, I'm not doing anything or, you know, consorting with anybody like my friends or anything. I'm totally disconnected from anything like that at this juncture, so I'm free to talk, like, at this juncture—"

Jake yells out, "Hey, lover boy! Don't forget we meet at my house around six thirty tomorrow morning!"

Cyril waves an impatient hand in acknowledgment: *Yes, yes, shut up!* The sound of his voice trails off as he stumbles away.

Behind him, Jake and Lucas Bixby start hooting like owls.

5:03 a.m. Saturday, December 8. Something rattles the windows of an upstairs bedroom at 44444 Agincourt Drive in Carrolton.

Is it an earthquake? A night monster?

No. It's just the sound of two sleeping, snorting, mouth-breathing boys.

Jake and Lucas Bixby are loud sleepers, but amazingly, they don't wake each other. They've been sharing the same bedroom for more than ten years, so each brother is used to the other's noises. Oddly enough, Lucas is a light sleeper. The slightest sound other than his brother's honking nose horn and gargling throat gunk can wake him from the deepest slumber.

Like that beeping sound, for instance. Listen. It's very faint. Hear it?

Lucas pops straight up with a piglike grunt.

"Hurgh?" he says.

He flings off his comforter and scrambles onto the floor. Jabbing his hands underneath the bed, he seizes his gadget backpack and yanks it out. The beeping is louder now.

"Jake!" he shrieks. *"Jake!"*

Jake, unlike his brother, is a heavy sleeper. And when we say *heavy*, we mean, like, multiple tonnage of sleep. So it will take more than a *"Jake!"* or two to drag Jake out of his dreamland. Lucas, being Jake's brother and room-mate, knows this, of course.

That's why he reaches onto the nightstand, grabs the water pistol, and unloads it into Jake's face.

Jake sits up slowly, face dripping. He looks around. Then he says, "Margo spit on the bananas."

"Jake! Wake up!"

Jake nods. "Okay," he says. He stretches and swings his legs over the edge of his bed. Then he looks up at Lucas. He says, "Don't eat the bananas, Chuck."

Lucas starts patting Jake's cheeks.

"Wake up, man!" he says. "The Omega Link!"

Jake smiles dopily.

Lucas starts patting harder. Actually, the "patting" is a bit more like slapping now.

"Ouch!" grunts Jake, suddenly grabbing one of his brother's wrists. Then he hears the beeping—finally. He forces his eyes wide open, sending deadly shards of sleep crust flying across the room.

Lucas ducks, then reaches down and pulls out the Omega Link. The display screen glows an eerie green, with black letters that read:

MOTHER NATURE
CROWN BASE VICTOR

"Quick!" whispers Jake. "Write it down before it disappears."

Lucas pulls out the Spy Gear casebook, unlatches the attached pen, and jots down the message.

"Got it!" he whispers back.

The moment Lucas says this, the gadget beeps again and the message disappears.

"Whew!" says Jake. "That was close."

"Mother Nature," reads Lucas from the casebook. "Crown Base Victor. What the hairball does that mean?"

Jake stares at it for a few seconds. Then he looks over at Lucas. They both nod.

"We need Lexi," say the brothers in unison.

The Omega Link beeps again.

Jake and Lucas stare at the display as another message appears, letter by letter—a simple, chilling message:

HIT BY AGENCY LIKELY
EXPECT LETHAL FORCE

Jake and Lucas sit, stunned. Then a final line appears on the screen:

ABANDON STONESHIP

⑩

LOCH NESS MONSTROSITY

6:15 a.m. Saturday, December 8. Birds twitter. At this ungodly hour, each cheery chirp sounds like the crack of a shotgun.

Suddenly, the doorbell rings at 44444 Agincourt Drive.

Upstairs, Mr. Bixby, forty, a tall, athletic-looking man, staggers to the landing. He rakes fingers through his blond hair, trying to reshape it into something that won't scare dogs or small children. Then he lurches downstairs to the front door.

Cyril Wong, looking like a member of some deranged hair cult, stands on the porch.

"Cyril," Mr. Bixby greets him, trying to smile but failing because the pain is too great. He steps backward to let Cyril enter.

"Mr. Bixby, sir," nods Cyril gravely.

Mr. Bixby claps Cyril on the shoulder as he walks by. He says, "I've always been a big supporter of the Boy Scouts."

Cyril stops. "I'm not a Boy Scout, sir," he says.

"You're not?"

"No."

"Then why the Boy Scout uniform?"

Cyril looks down. "This is a hockey jersey, sir."

"Hockey?"

"Yes. Hockey." Cyril swings an imaginary hockey stick. "Like, you whack pucks into a net, then get into really gruesome fights?"

Mr. Bixby slaps his cheeks, trying to wake up. Looking confused, he says, "When did the Boy Scouts start a hockey team?"

Cyril says, "Is Jake up yet?"

"I don't know."

Cyril nods and walks into the kitchen. Mr. Bixby shuffles like a zombie after him. Cyril goes to the cupboard, grabs a box of cereal, and pours flakes directly into his mouth. Mr. Bixby collapses onto a stool at the breakfast bar.

"So what have you been up to, Cyril?" asks Mr. Bixby, head in his hands.

Crunching flakes, Cyril says, "Nothing, sir, other than saving the world from evildoers." He puts the cereal box away. "But of course that's *everybody's* job these days."

"Not mine," mumbles Mr. Bixby. "My job is to tell people what they want, and then sell it to them."

"I hope to get a job in marketing someday too, sir," says Cyril.

Mr. Bixby puts his head down on the counter. "Somehow, I'm sure you will."

Cyril nods. "Well, I've really learned a lot here, Mr. Bixby, thanks," he says. "I think I'll, you know, head up to Jake's room now."

"Say hello for me, will you?" says Mr. Bixby, closing his eyes.

"Good night, sir," says Cyril.

Jake and Lucas Bixby, as you might imagine, are both *intensely* awake and ready to roll. Indeed, the intensity is so thick you could cut it with a Bolivian machete. Cyril has to push through about two inches of raw intenseness just to get into the bedroom.

"Cyril!" shout Jake and Lucas in unison when they see him.

"*Aaagh!*" Cyril screams.

"Sorry," says Jake.

"Guys!" gasps Cyril, holding his heart, which just jumped out of his chest. He reinserts it and says, "Ramp it down *just a notch* there, would you?"

"Dude!" says Jake. "We got new Omega messages this morning."

Lucas scrambles to his backpack and yanks out the Spy Gear casebook. As Cyril sits on Jake's bed, Lucas opens the book to the spot and plops it on Cyril's lap. Grimacing, Cyril reads the messages.

"Abandon Stoneship," he says as he reads the last message line. "Huh." He looks up at Jake. "The Agency is going to hit it with lethal force. Hey, that sounds like fun!"

Jake shrugs. "What do you think?" he asks.

Cyril stands up. "I think we should lay low for a while," he says. "Catch up on reading. Maybe raise some chickens." He nods.

The boys hear a scrabbling sound from the drainpipe just outside the bedroom window. They watch placidly as someone slowly jacks up the window. There is a brief pause. Then Lexi dives in headfirst. She tucks into a quick somersault as she hits the floor, then completes the spin by popping up to her feet, arms raised up high, all in one fluid motion.

"Hey," she says.

"Hey," say the guys.

Lucas holds out the casebook to Lexi. She takes it and reads the Omega messages.

"Mother Nature," she says. "That was one of the big trees."

Jake and Lucas look at each other.

"Of course!" Lucas nods. "Mother Nature! She was that really huge Douglas fir, remember?"

"Right," says Jake. "As I recall, Mother was near one of the interior trails of the arboretum."

"So what does 'Crown Base Victor' mean?" asks Cyril.

Lucas says, "If it's a 'base,' maybe it's some kind of meeting or gathering place?"

Everyone looks at Lexi. But this time she just shrugs. "No clue," she says.

"Victor is the designation for the letter V in the military alphabet," says Jake.

"So maybe . . . V as in Viper?" suggests Lucas.

"Maybe."

"Hmmm," says Cyril. "But a victor is also a *winner*. And a crown is something that royalty wears—like, a king. *Or perhaps a queen.*" He raises his eyebrows and gives everyone a significant look.

Jake, Lexi, and Lucas wait.

Finally Cyril says, "Mother Nature? A queen? Wears a crown? Never loses? Get it? Get it?"

"No," says Jake. He looks at Lexi.

"Nope," she says. She looks at Lucas.

"Not me," says Lucas.

Cyril says, "Oh, *yeah*? Well, I don't get it either, so *ha!*"

Lucas takes the Spy Gear casebook from Lexi and flips back to the "No Omega" note glued next to a sketch of the snake-eyes dice. He points and says, "Remember, we're not supposed to trust the link anymore. Especially if it's true that Viper has a working quantum computer capable of hacking into secure com-link networks."

"Right," says Jake. "And you know, maybe I'm goofy, but these messages seem like they're from two different sources again."

"Exactly!" says Lucas. "The Mother Nature message seems to direct us back to the Old North Stand. But the 'lethal force' message wants to scare us away from Stoneship altogether."

"So which message is from the Agency mole, and which one is from Viper?" asks Jake.

Lucas glances at his watch.

"Whoa, it's getting late," he says. "We've only got twenty-five minutes to set up for the Wolf Pack meeting at Loch Ness." He slips the Omega Link back into his gadget backpack, then slings the pack over his shoulders. "We can analyze this Omega input more thoroughly later."

"Okay," Jake says. "Mount up, platoon."

Team Spy Gear troops downstairs and out the front door.

7:04 a.m. A minivehicle resembling a lobster on wheels hums quietly down an asphalt walkway on the Loch Ness Elementary School playground. It stops at the feet of Lucas Bixby.

"Test run complete," whispers Lucas, who crouches behind a hedgerow next to the path holding a remote controller.

Behind him, the rest of Team Spy Gear stays low behind the hedgerow too. Jake gives Lucas a thumbs-up sign. Cyril pumps a fist. Lexi points at the mobile device, a Spy Robot.

"That thing rocks!" whispers Lexi, eyes bright. "It's totally nuclear."

Lucas grins. "I heartily concur with that analysis," he says.

He reaches into his gadget backpack and pulls out a spherical Spy Bug. The electronic bug has three prongs on its base. Lucas slides these into three matching grooves atop the Spy Robot. The fit is perfect.

"These things are engineered to work together," explains Lucas in hushed tones. He pushes a button on the Spy Bug; the top half of the sphere flips up to become a sonic dish with an antenna. "See? When you put the Robot and the Bug together, it becomes a mobile listening platform."

Lucas clips the Spy Bug's receiver unit on his belt and slips its earbud into his ear. Now he can hear whatever the Spy Bug's sonic dish picks up. Meanwhile, Jake uses an extendable viewing scope called a Micro Periscope to peek over the hedgerow.

"Okay, Brill just arrived," says Jake as he peers through

the scope. "I think the pack meeting is about to start. Better deploy now."

"Roger that," replies Lucas.

He picks up the remote control unit for the Spy Robot, adjusts its wire antenna a bit, and then steers the radio-controlled rover down the asphalt path.

"Wait!" says Cyril.

Lucas halts the rover. "What?" he asks.

"It needs a name," says Cyril.

"It's the Spy Robot," says Lucas.

"No, no," says Cyril, scowling. "That's not a name. I'm talking something like, I don't know, Bob."

"Bob?"

"Yes. Bob."

"Why?"

"Why not?" says Cyril.

Lucas just looks at Cyril for a moment. A sudden gust of wind whips Cyril's hair around. It looks like Persian cats wrestling. In the distance, a moose trumpets in the Yukon. Flocks of vultures circle around a carcass on the Serengeti Plain. Three men push a boat into the Ganges River.

Then Lucas nods.

"Bob it is," he says.

"*Now* we're talking," says Cyril, rubbing his hands together.

Bob continues to roll down the walkway, which loops completely around the playground of Loch Ness

Elementary School. Lucas steers so that Bob hugs the raised brick edging on the walkway's inner curve; thus Bob can't be seen from inside the playground.

Brill has convened his meeting on the Loch Ness handball court. This location is cleverly chosen. The court is enclosed on three sides by high walls, with the open end facing the back of the school building. This cuts off not only viewing but (more important) listening angles. With the Wolf Pack gathered inside the sound buffer of the walls, none of Team Spy Gear's distant listening devices—in particular, the Spy Supersonic Ear, with its high-powered sound amplification dish—can eavesdrop. Nor can a human spy creep up to the meeting without being spotted by two Wolf Pack sentries posted at the court's open end.

However, the playground's walkway loop runs right past the open end of the handball court. And the edging is high enough to hide Bob.

"But wait, Bob's antenna sticks up over the edging," points out Jake.

"It's just a wire, pretty hard to see," says Lucas, thumbing the radio controls. "But I'll go slower as soon as the rover—"

"Bob," interjects Cyril.

Lucas gives him a look. "—as soon as *Bob* gets closer to the sentries."

As the Spy Robot rolls closer to its listening target,

Lucas leans out from the hedgerow a little to see better. He picks up the first bits of chatter in the Spy Bug earpiece. Brill's harsh voice brays loudly above the others.

Okay, shut up, you [censored], shouts Brill. **Listen up!**

Lucas halts Bob for a second. Then, when he sees the two Wolf Pack sentries turn toward Brill, Lucas drives the rover closer until it reaches the open end of the court where the pack is gathered.

Next to Lucas, Cyril holds up a pad of paper and a pencil. "Ready," he says.

Lucas nods. He starts repeating what he hears Brill saying to the pack.

"First, he's making them all recite the Wolf Pack pledge," he says. He listens a moment. Then: "Wow, that's lame."

"Can you repeat it for us?" asks Jake.

"I could, but then I'd die of mad embarrassment," says Lucas.

"Cat says the Wolf Pack is an insult to wolves," says Cyril. "She says wolves are actually really cool dudes."

"Okay, here we go," says Lucas. "Meeting to order."

Cyril puts his pencil to the pad.

"Brill says it's time to make their move," repeats Lucas. "He's says it's time the Bixbys and their friends know the bloody wrath of the Wolf Pack."

Jake hears the pack howling and yipping with delight at this across the playground. He exchanges a glance with Cyril, who looks like he's trying to swallow something large and sour.

"Brill says tonight's the night," repeats Lucas, listening intently.

Again, the pack erupts in howls. Cyril transcribes quickly as Lucas speaks.

"Now Wilson is talking," Lucas continues. "Handing out tactical assignments. Five o'clock tonight. Meet where the Bixbys always enter and exit Stoneship Woods." He listens some more. "Brill plans to lead a large recon party of twenty troops directly into the forest, with Wilson in charge of a rear guard unit posted on the county road."

Cyril furiously scribbles all this down. He says, "Hey, if Brill and the pack enter Stoneship there, they'll find the access road."

Jake nods, frowning. "And that will lead them right to the warehouse."

"And that will be bad," says Lexi angrily.

"Yes. Very bad."

"As bad as it gets."

Across the playground, sounds of canine growling and mewling can be heard.

"What's going on now, bro?" asks Jake.

"Interesting," says Lucas. "Brill says anybody's free to chicken out right now, if they're afraid of all the Stoneship ghost stories." He smiles as he listens further.

"Ooooh, *big* mistake. He just mentioned the Wild Axman of Killicut County."

Now the whining and yipping in the handball court grows louder and more uncertain.

"The Wild Axman," says Cyril, looking ill. "Great! I finally stopped dreaming about him last year."

"Cyril, that's a legend," says Jake. "The Axman isn't real."

Cyril stares at Jake. "Oh, you *know* this, do you?"

Jake rolls his eyes.

Suddenly Lucas laughs. "Somebody just asked about the barking tree squids," he says. "Now all the old legends are coming out." He listens, nodding. "Yes, the Burmese tusk rats. The killer weevils. But Brill says he's not afraid of stupid ghost stories. Asserting his alpha status quite well." He shakes his head. "I have to hand it to him. He's very effective, in a demented sort of way."

Now a loud, long, lingering howl rises.

"That's it," croaks Cyril. "The Final Howl."

"Here they come!" whispers Jake, watching through his Micro Periscope.

"Get down!"

Team Spy Gear ducks low. They can hear the tramping, snorting, and snarling of the pack as it moves down the path just on the other side of the hedgerow. After a few seconds, the sound diminishes to silence. Jake carefully peers over the top of the bush with his periscope, and then proclaims the coast clear.

As Team Spy Gear emerges and crosses the play-ground to retrieve Bob the Spy Robot, Jake glances over at his brother.

Lucas is smiling big.

"Getting some ideas?" asks Jake.

"Oh, they just keep popping into my head," says Lucas. "I can't help it. It's like a disease."

Jake nods, grinning. "And I'll bet I know what at least *one* of your ideas might be."

Lucas shows his teeth.

4:34 p.m., later the same day.

At the Carrolton Mall, Marco stands next to an old, beat-up silver Mazda. In his hand, he holds an Agent Tracker seeker unit. He gazes down at it; its arc lights flash red, indicating that the tracker bug he planted on the Mall Security car is nearby. Sure enough, as he peers across the lot, he sees the familiar white vehicle parked outside the Food Court.

Marco tosses the Agent Tracker unit onto the front seat of the Mazda and flips open a brand-new, fancy-looking cell phone. He presses a speed-dial button. Then he holds the phone to his ear, watching the Food Court entrance doors.

After a second he says, "This phone you gave me has an echo. But yes, the mole's here. I tracked him with your tracker gizmo."

Marco listens to someone speak. Through the sleek Agency-issue phone, the voice on the other end sounds remarkably like a Corellian cyborg, or maybe just someone speaking through a digital LP filter mask, it's hard to tell. But then Marco cuts him off, saying, "Wait. Here he comes."

Now the bald head of Dr. Hork appears, gleaming in the bright December sun as he pushes through the Food Court doors. The same two burly guards wait to escort him into the car.

Marco lowers his phone, watching Dr. Hork carefully. The fleshy scientist in the blue lab coat carries a take-out salad in a clear plastic container in one hand. In the other hand he holds a shiny red apple. He climbs into the backseat of the Mall Security car. The two guards slip into the backseat too, one on each side.

Then the white car drives off.

Marco raises the phone to his ear again.

"Okay, the mole is away," he says. He glances down at his watch. "Hey, I gotta go."

He flips the phone shut.

Marco slides into the old Mazda, starts up the coughing motor, and drives away, spewing smoke from the tailpipe.

4:53 p.m. Cyril shivers on the shoulder of County Road 44, about two hundred yards north of the old access road into Stoneship Woods. It's not even five o'clock yet, but dusk is already gathering, cold and gray in the east. Remember, the winter solstice is less than two weeks away. The days are short.

"This isn't fair," says Cyril into the slim mouthpiece of his headset.

Hey, you got the fun job, replies Jake via Spy Link.

"Fun?" says Cyril. "I have to look into hungry lupine eyes and lie like a dirty sock."

You can do it, says Jake. **Remember, just act like you're really afraid.**

"Act?" says Cyril. "Why would I need to do that?"

Exactly, says Jake. **Just be yourself.**

"I'd rather not," says Cyril.

Jake laughs. **Don't forget,** he says, **you've got backup dogs. So don't panic.**

"You know, Jake," says Cyril philosophically, "I always figured that if there was a planetary war, and we all had to fight off an invasion of Nardok trolls or something, I'd be a decoy. My job would be to lure the monsters."

Why do you think that? asks Jake.

"Because I was born to lure monsters."

Jake laughs again. Then he says, **All Go Team units are in position and ready to roll.**

"Roger," says Cyril bleakly. He turns to gaze north-west up the road.

Hey, it could be worse, says Lucas in Cyril's ear. **You could be in the peasant army. You know, the human fodder thrown at impregnable enemy positions in order to buy time for the elite divisions?**

Cyril brightens. "True," he says. He sees movement up the road. "Uh-oh, here they come. I see the gleam of green eyes." His voice deepens. "Unit One, we have one hundred meters to engagement, over."

Roger that, says Jake. **Go Team, be advised that we have initial contact with tangos in thirty. Prepare to execute Operation Barking Thunder.**

Cyril takes a deep breath. He stretches his arms overhead to loosen up, bounces lightly on his feet a few times, and throws a few shadow punches. Down the road, the snarling mob approaches.

Cyril takes another deep breath.

Then he starts screaming.

What a master! whispers Lucas Bixby via Spy Link to his brother. **You'd think he was actually terrified, given that performance.**

Jake, sitting in the low branches of a small cottonwood tree, stifles a nervous laugh. He can hear the crunching of twigs as a sizeable enemy platoon pushes through the low foliage below him.

"I've got significant activity here," whispers Jake. "Looks like Cyril's bringing them your way."

Roger, answers Lucas. *We've got the clearing fully prepped and ready.*

"Good," Jake whispers. "Let's just hope Cyril makes it there alive."

Jake carefully pushes aside a branch for a better view. Below, just a few yards from his tree, Cyril leads Brill Joseph and a column of Wolf Pack boys along a dark, narrow path. Jake hears Cyril's voice below and also via the Spy Link.

"This way!" babbles Cyril. "Quick!"

Then Jake sees Brill suddenly grab Cyril hard by the back of the neck. With great difficulty, Jake stifles the urge to drop from the tree and leap on Brill's back. He grits his teeth and watches Brill shake Cyril's head a few times.

"Why do you come in here?" hisses Brill.

"For fun," answers Cyril.

"What could possibly be *fun* in these woods?" snarls Brill.

"Well, the tusk rats are kind of cute to watch," says Cyril. "Until they attack, of course. We usually wear hockey masks when we go rat-watching." He points down the path. "Can we hurry, please? My poor friends the Bixbys ran into this clearing." He adds deep concern to his voice. "I'm pretty sure they're entangled in weevil webs. *We gotta get 'em out, fellas!*"

He starts running up the path. Brill shouts, "Wait for us, you [censored] mophead geek!"

Brill and the Wolf Pack chase Cyril into the clearing just ahead. Cyril leads them toward a dark clump of small

Gambel oak trees. Suddenly, a shrill, high-pitched barking begins somewhere up high. As Brill's minions pour into the clearing, more chirping barks can be heard in the trees all around.

"What the [censored] is that?" demands Brill, scanning the surrounding branches.

Cyril skids to a halt, looking scared.

"Wait!" he whispers dramatically. "I *know* that bark!"

"What is it?" Brill yells.

Cyril gives Brill a wide-eyed look of terror. Then he reaches out to clasp Brill's shoulder.

"Tree squids!" he gasps hoarsely.

The weird squawking barks sound creepy, high-pitched, unnatural—and they come from at least a dozen different directions. Now a few high branches shake on the clearing's perimeter.

Brill and several Wolf Pack boys start edging away from the trees. They gather in the center of the clearing. As they do so, Cyril slinks away from the group and huddles near a bush at the far side of the clearing. He puts a finger to his Spy Link earpiece.

"The crow flies at midnight," he whispers.

Suddenly, a shower of tiny wormlike bugs falls from the sky into the center of the clearing, hitting the Wolf Pack like hundreds of slimy raindrops.

"*Weevils!*" shrieks Cyril.

The pack starts howling in fear. Brill, wiping insects

off his face, tries to lead a wild scramble from the clearing to the trail.

"Run!" shrieks Cyril. "Get out! Get out before they start *weaving their webs!*"

Wild animal panic grips the clearing now. Boys crawl over other boys. Somebody even claws past Brill, knocking the pack's alpha wolf into a thorny elderberry bush. He howls in pain. Then Brill scrambles to his feet and follows his minions up the path.

Nearby, Jake drops from his tree post, as do Lucas and Lexi. They rush across the clearing to Cyril.

"Nice shot with the worms!" says Cyril to Lucas. They slap hands. "Right on the money, dude!"

"Quick, let's follow them!" says Jake, grinning. "I don't want to miss the grand finale."

Team Spy Gear rushes to the trail opening and sprints down the path. Up ahead, the intensity of howls and screams lessens a bit. Leading the way, Jake reaches the trailhead at the forest's edge, then drops behind some high prairie grass. The others join him.

Out on County Road 44, about half of the Wolf Pack runs screaming up the road to the north. But the other half seems to be regrouping under Brill. They've joined with Wilson's rear guard unit posted on the road. Jake can hear Brill's panicked voice telling Wilson about the weevil attack. Wilson's reply is skeptical, and for a tense moment it appears the Wolf Pack's alpha wolf position may be up for grabs.

But then a low, bone-chilling moan rises from the forest, just down the tree line from Team Spy Gear. Brill, Wilson, and the other boys freeze with fear. They look at the spot in the trees. The moan grows louder.

"Go, Cyril!" whispers Jake. "Now!"

Cyril pops out of the high grass, running toward the Wolf Pack remnants. The moan from the trees transforms into a hideous, throat-rattling Shriek of Cold Death. And just as Cyril reaches Brill, a wild-haired, deranged, blood-gargling maniac bursts from the tree line. High above his tangled mane of hair, the fiend waves a huge, double-bladed ax.

"My God!" yells Cyril, pointing. "It's . . . *the Wild Axman of Killicut County!*"

The gory madman runs toward the boys, roaring like a beast.

The boys shriek and run.

Cyril runs after them, but lets the pack pull ahead. His wild sprint slows to a run, then to a jog. Then he falls to the ground, chuckling. The Wild Axman, still roaring, runs past Cyril. He jogs up the road a few more yards, barking and howling horribly. Then he stops.

In the distance, the last of the screaming Wolf Pack disappears around the bend in County Road 44.

The Wild Axman trudges back to Cyril and helps him to his feet.

"You were a little too realistic for my taste," says Cyril, grinning.

"Sorry," says the Wild Axman.

Now Jake, Lexi, and Lucas jog up to them. "You know, in silhouette, you two look like long-lost brothers," says Jake.

"Except I'm not ugly," says Cyril.

The Wild Axman whacks him upside the head, but in that brotherly way that only hurts a little bit. Then Marco turns to Lucas and hands over the ax.

"This is an excellent ax," he says.

"I knew you'd like it."

Marco says, "How'd you do all that barking? It sounded like dozens of inhuman little things."

Lucas holds up a small, cylinder-shaped gadget. "Spy Voice Trap," he says. "Records a six-second loop triggered by a motion sensor. Lexi and I put about ten of them up in the trees, all aimed down at the clearing. Every time someone moved down there, well—" He turns on the Voice Trap gizmo and waves his hand in front of it, triggering a playback of high-pitched yelps. "That's actually a barking seal, sped up to double time." He grins. "I got it off the Internet."

Suddenly, Lexi gasps.

"What?" asks Jake.

She points up at the towering trees of the Old North Stand, looming high to the northwest of them.

Colored lights flicker in the high branches.

(11)

FIRST FLOOR

The arboretum entry gate lies shattered on the rutted road leading into the Old North Stand. Team Spy Gear gazes soberly at the wreckage—well, except for Cyril, who keeps spinning to check behind him.

"You know, whatever direction you face, half of the world is *still* behind you," says Cyril. "I really hate that."

"Poor species design," Lucas agrees.

"Come on," says Jake. "The trailhead isn't far." He pulls the arboretum map out of his pocket. "I say we head straight for Mother Nature."

Okay, I'm upstairs, says Marco via Spy Link. No sign of lethal force here at Stoneship. He chortles. If that happens, I'll be sure to let you know.

Cyril looks sullen. "Remote operational control from HQ is supposed to be *my* job," he says.

"Sorry, man," says Jake. "We have to take the lethal force warnings seriously."

"But even Marco thinks that Omega warning was just some Viper shenanigans," complains Cyril. "You know, breaking into our link with a quantum burst to sow fear and confusion."

"Maybe," says Jake. He leads the team across the trailhead clearing. "But I think it's better if we stick together tonight." He looks at Cyril. "For recon purposes."

"I'm not a field man," grumbles Cyril.

"Come on, dude," says Jake. "You might surprise yourself."

"Or I might surprise the paramedics," says Cyril. *"Hey, look, the kid's still twitching!"*

Using Jake's map, the team navigates quickly down the trails to the towering Douglas fir named Mother Nature. Lexi approaches the placard near the trunk. "Yes, it's her," she says with reverence. She leans in closer and reads: "Mother Nature is one hundred eighty-nine feet tall and twenty-one feet around, with a crown spread of eighty-eight feet. Wow."

Jake nods and gazes at the massive, gnarly trunk. Then he frowns and looks quickly over at Lexi. "Wait. Did you say 'crown spread'?"

"That's what it says," nods Lexi.

"What *is* a crown spread?" asks Jake.

"I'm not sure," says Lexi.

Lucas snaps his fingers. "Crown!" he says. "The Omega message!"

Jake quickly flips open the arboretum brochure, a slick, six-page booklet with the map and information on the arboretum trees. The back page has a glossary of tree terms.

"Here it is," says Jake. "'Crown. The upper part of a tree, including branches and foliage.'"

"So what's a 'crown base,' then?" asks Lucas.

And thus we enter the Great Web, crackles Marco's voice via Spy Link. Crown base, tree anatomy. T-minus ten seconds to Google.

"Dang it," says Cyril. "That's *my* job!" He looks over at Jake. "Dude, I should go join him at HQ."

No, no, no, says Marco quickly before Jake can speak. I prefer, uh, to be alone here, you know, to work alone.

And gosh, here's where several interesting things happen, all within seconds of one another.

As Marco voices his desire to be alone, the HQ workstation computer beeps, indicating completion of its online search. With another click, Marco brings up a text file onscreen: a definition of "crown base" from the U.S. Forestry Service Web site. He reads it quietly and nods. Then he reaches to the console and flips a switch, cutting the Spy Link channel.

"Got it," he says.

"Let me see," says a nasally voice behind him.

Marco slides his chair sideways. A very short man in a black suit, black gloves, and sunglasses steps up to the monitor. He leans over to read the onscreen text. Then he puts a black-gloved finger to his ear.

"Alpha units, let's get to that gate, all possible speed," he says. "Stand by, Charlie One and Two, no location lock yet, stand by, repeat, stand by." There's more than a hint of self-importance in the agent's tone. He tugs on his black gloves, adjusting them. Then he holds out his hands, giving them an appraising glance. Clearly, this fellow loves his gloved look. He loves being the mysterious Gloved Agent.

Marco looks up sullenly. "Can I *answer* them now?" he asks.

The Gloved Agent nods solemnly and steps back. He gestures to the console.

"Proceed," he says.

Again, his air of authority seems a bit overdone. Marco rolls his eyes, then slides his chair back to the console and flips a switch to open the Spy Link channel again. Immediately, he hears a commotion—several kids talking at once.

—hear that? Jake is saying. Where—?

In the tree! shouts Cyril at the same time. Holy Smithsonian!

Look out!

What was that?

It landed over there!

Where?

There. See it?

Now let's wind the clock back just a few seconds.

As the agent at Stoneship HQ calls in his Alpha units, Dr. Hork, the scientist in the blue lab coat, is eating in a laboratory filled with a stunning array of instruments. He sits at a desk near the lab's only window. Gloomily, he forks salad into his mouth from a clear plastic take-out container.

As he chews, Dr. Hork stares out the open window at a mosaic of fir tree branches.

He sets down his plastic fork and grabs an apple from the table. His teeth tear crisply through the glossy red skin. Suddenly, a huge man wearing a mall security guard uniform bursts through a nearby door, gun drawn. His head is shaved and gleaming; it looks polished. His eyes are hidden behind the blue lenses of his sunglasses.

"We have a situation," says the guard calmly but with a hard, no-nonsense tone. "Code Red, immediate evac."

"Whaa—?" mumbles Dr. Hork around the mouthful of apple flesh.

The guard, wearing a com-link earpiece, listens to it for a second, then steps quickly to a glass case near the doorway. He gives it a quick punch with his Mauser pistol, shattering the glass.

"What are you doing?" shouts Dr. Hork. "Are you *insane?*"

The guard punches buttons on a numeric keypad inside the case. As he does, Dr. Hork leaps angrily to his feet. He tosses the apple through the window just as the guard finishes his keypad input. A loud buzzer sounds. A message on the keypad screen flashes red: *SD System Armed.*

"Sierra Delta activated," he says into a button mike on his lapel.

Stunned, Dr. Hork gestures around the lab. "My work!" he exclaims. "This is my *work!*"

"This is just relocation," says the guard calmly. "Please gather the critical data immediately."

Dr. Hork slides open a desk drawer and pulls out a silver data disk. "I have everything right here," he says. "But what about the prototype? The lasers?" He gestures at a large rack of instrumentation on the opposite wall. "The ion trap alone will take months, maybe *years* to rebuild and recalibrate—"

"Sir!" interrupts the guard.

"Yes?"

The guard merely waves the Mauser pistol toward the door—a gentle wave.

"After you, sir," he says.

* * *

Jake stares up into the branches of Mother Nature. "That was definitely a loud buzz," he says. "We all heard it, right?"

Nearby, Lexi picks up the shiny object that just thudded into the ground after ricocheting off limbs above. "It's an apple," she says.

"Are you kidding?" says Lucas. He goes over to examine the fruit.

"So what was that buzz?" asks Jake, still looking up.

Cyril looks uneasy. "Some sort of tree snort," he says. "Or maybe a hornet."

Jake stares at him. "A hornet?"

Cyril shrugs. "A *big* hornet," he says. "Possibly."

"Sounded like an alarm to me," says Jake. "Like, an alarm buzzer."

Cyril nods. "That's possible too, if you have the right kind of imagination."

Nearby, Lucas examines the apple. Then he looks up at the tree.

"This isn't an apple tree," he says. "It's a Douglas fir."

"Why would an apple fall from a Douglas fir?" asks Lexi.

Lucas examines the apple closer. "It's pretty dinged up from hitting stuff on the way down," he says. "But look at this gouge." He points to a big round gash.

"Hey, those are teeth marks," says Lexi.

"Teeth marks?" says Jake.

Hey, little people, calls Marco via Spy Link. **Hello? You there? I got your tree info.**

"What?" replies Jake. In the commotion, everyone has forgotten about this.

Crown base, reads Marco. **The base of a tree's crown is defined as the lowest complete branch whorl or major branch that forms part of the canopy.**

Team Spy Gear exchanges looks.

Can you see anything up in the lowest branches of that big mother tree? asks Marco.

All eyes turn upward.

Minutes later Lexi grabs another limb and hoists herself onto it. She looks over at the next closest shoot, six feet diagonally up Mother Nature's trunk.

"Don't try that!" calls Jake from the ground, twenty feet below. "Lexi?"

Lexi looks down at Jake.

Jake says, "I know you're amazing and indestructible, but—"

She jumps.

"Aaaarrgh!" yells Cyril.

Lexi catches the next limb with both hands and her legs swing forward. As she swings back, she adds momentum and whips her body upward, locking her arms. This pivots her upper body above the branch. Lexi swings her legs up and stands on the branch, leaning into the trunk.

Cyril falls over backward. He lies on the ground with his arms splayed out.

"I can't take this," he says quietly.

Lexi, beaming, calls down, "That was the worst one. I can reach the crown easy from here."

Mother Nature's crown base—that is, its lowest full spread of branches—is a full forty feet off the ground. But below that, smaller limbs (which *everyone* knows are called "epicormic shoots") jut from the trunk at irregular intervals. Some are just stubby remnants; others are no more than thick knots in the trunk. Naturally, Lexi sees the whole thing as an exhilarating climbing puzzle.

"Yeah, looks like a good route the rest of the way up," calls Lucas. "But dude, use that rope like we discussed, will you? You're scaring the blue blazes out of me."

Lexi wraps a rope several times around her waist and ties an expert knot. Then she secures the other end to the next highest branch.

And up she goes.

The boys watch nervously as Lexi clambers from shoot to shoot (untying and retying the rope each time) until she finally reaches the big, bushy boughs of the crown base, forty feet up. The Douglas fir's canopy is thick; Lexi grabs hold of a branch and completely disappears, quick as a monkey.

The boys exchange looks.

"I hate this part," says Lucas. "You know, the waiting."

They wait.

Time slows to an excruciating crawl.

Then, via Spy Link, Lexi says: **Oh, my, God.**

Suddenly, there is a low hum. Then a whining machine-like noise.

"Lexi?" shouts everyone, including you and everybody in Waukegan, Illinois.

Then, amazingly, one of the biggest branches starts to swivel downward. It drops as if somehow hinged where it connects to the tree trunk.

"That branch looks, I don't know, *hinged* somehow," says Lucas.

"Yes, where it connects to the tree trunk," notes Cyril. "See how it swivels downward?"

"Yes, I see!" exclaims Jake. "I see the hingelike connector, which causes the swiveling motion of the branch as it, like, swivels."

The boys glare at the author. The author shrugs and backs away from the keyboard, setting them free.

As the big branch lowers with a mechanical hum, it reveals the square, camouflaged bottom of a lift platform up in the crown base. With a hydraulic hiss, the platform starts to move downward. It drops smoothly all the way to the ground.

Lexi, eyes afire, rides the lift. Her fingers rest on a small control panel.

"All aboard," she says.

Lucas whoops. He slings his gadget backpack over the lift's railing, leaps over himself, and whacks palms hard with Lexi. *"Yes!"* he says with gusto. Hey, we all know how deeply Lucas loves mechanisms. For Lucas, something like a turbo-lift makes life totally, intensely vibrant and dazzling and brilliant.

He says, "Can I operate it?"

Grinning, Lexi steps aside.

Jake and Cyril hop aboard too. The turbo-lift's not large—big enough to hold maybe six people. Like the lift's bottom, its floor is painted an intricate camouflage pattern resembling fir branches. A sturdy waist-high railing runs around the edge. As Jake quickly reports these findings to Marco, Lucas presses a control-panel button. The lift rises.

"Somebody pinch me," says Lucas, almost dazed with delight.

Jake looks up. "But what are we riding *up* to?" he asks.

Stay on your toes, children, cautions Marco.

"I found the lift at the crown base, but its track keeps going up the tree trunk," says Lexi.

Jake nods, still gazing upward. "So who's *up* there?"

"The secret lab?" asks Lexi, frowning.

Cyril looks ill. "Ah yes, the bad guys," he whispers. "How quickly we forget."

As they ascend into the canopy, the big tree limb that lowered earlier now rises beneath the lift, locking back into place.

"Great goats!" says Lucas. He leans over the railing to look down at the spot where the branch intersects the trunk. "That *is* hinged. Dude, it's an artificial, mechanical Douglas fir branch!"

Up, up they go.

Night is falling fast now. Mother Nature's canopy is so thick and bushy that little is visible in any direction other than straight up. The turbo-lift slides quietly up a well-hidden, recessed metal track bolted to the gargantuan trunk. It rises toward a square opening in a wooden landing maybe a hundred feet up. This landing rings around the trunk in a perfect circle.

"Wow!" says Lucas, gazing up at it.

Cyril plops down on the lift's floor.

"What are you doing there, bud?" asks Jake with a hint of amusement.

"I figure they'll hit us with phasers when we arrive," says Cyril, gesturing weakly upward. "Set to stun, if we're lucky."

"That's why you're sitting down," Jake says.

"Yes," says Cyril.

"So you won't fall and, like, break your hair."

"Precisely," says Cyril. Now he stretches out on his back. "Ah, that's even better."

Slowly, *very* slowly, the lift rises toward the hole in the wooden landing.

Back at HQ, Marco listens intently to Team Spy Gear's reports via the Spy Link channel. With a crease of concern growing across his brow, he wraps his huge hand around the console microphone to muffle it. He turns to the Gloved Agent.

"Are they safe up there?" he asks.

The agent clasps his black gloves in front of him and tilts his head as if considering the question. Finally, he says, "Is anybody ever really *safe*, my friend?"

Irritated, Marco says, "How about a straight answer, Jack?"

The Gloved Agent looks a bit offended, but he rubs his gloves together thoughtfully. "Are they safe? Well, now. The straight answer, *Jack*, would have to be: We don't know yet." After a dramatic pause, he adds, "For all we know, your little people have discovered the Harvey P. Wilks Memorial Treetop Playground."

"Or maybe they found a secret quantum computer lab," says Marco.

Another pause. Then: "Well, now. We don't know that yet."

Marco nods. "It's amazing what you guys don't know," he says. "Whatever they pay you, it's *way* too much."

The Gloved Agent's eyes flare. "I don't think you're in any position to crack wise with me," he says with nasal menace.

"Hey," says Marco. "You're willing to let innocent kids walk into the claws of some dark thug."

The agent scoffs. "You know so little," he says with disgust.

"Really?" says Marco darkly. "Then educate me."

The black gloves seem barely capable of restraint now. "First of all, Viper is no mere *thug*," says the agent with thinly veiled hatred. "Even calling him a threat to national security would be . . . an understatement."

"Really," says Marco, sounding unimpressed. "He didn't seem that scary to me."

"Did you ever meet him?"

"In person? No."

"No," repeats the Gloved Agent with a hint of contempt. "No, of course not. So your role as *pawn* wouldn't allow you much vision or perspective now, would it?"

"Oh, so he's a big bad guy?" says Marco.

The agent nods. "Bigger than you can imagine."

Marco, hand still clasped over the console mike, points angrily at it with his other hand. "Then they *are* in danger."

"Our *mole* is in danger; there is no doubt of that," sniffs the agent. "But your diminutive colleagues? I don't think so." He pauses again for effect. "Only if they get in the way."

Marco takes a deep breath, staring with undisguised anger at the little man. "Only if they get in the way?" he repeats.

"Yes!" says the Gloved Agent with sudden intensity. "You see, my hirsute friend, this is an operation we've been arranging for *years*. And nothing, *nothing*, is more important than its successful *execution*." He speaks the last word with a little too much relish.

Marco stares at the agent for a moment. Then he says, "Stop calling me friend."

The agent nods. "As you wish," he says.

"By the way," says Marco, "where's the big dark guy?" He glances out the plate-glass windows, scanning the warehouse floor. "I don't see him stumbling around anywhere." Then he gives the agent a sly look. "Isn't he your superior?"

The Gloved Agent winces at that last word. He looks off into the distance. "We all have our *roles*," he says. "But right now, *I* am in charge of field operations, and that's all you need to know."

Marco smiles grimly. "Understood," he says. "But, just in case, maybe you should have coffee ready for the boss when he gets back." Still gripping the mike, he points with his free hand at a coffeemaker hung with cobwebs at the far end of the console desk.

The agent stares at the appliance. He takes a deep breath.

"Very funny," he says.

Marco turns to the console. He shakes his dreadlocks.

"They're walking into something bad," he says quietly. "A trap."

"Unlikely," says the agent. "More likely they'll find the

place deserted." A hint of distress ripples across his face, like something moving just beneath the surface of a dark pond. "I fear our foe's quantum capabilities have given him access to your little friends and their, shall we say, *thinking*, if one could call it that."

"You mean he's tapped the Spy Link channel," says Marco. He looks again at his hand on the console mike. Then he narrows his eyes. "So what can I tell them?"

"Tell them to move slowly and report everything they see," says the agent. "My people are ready to move quickly, but we don't have, well, *full* access to the complex. Not yet, anyway."

"In other words, you haven't figured out how to get up there," says Marco with a grim look.

"Well, your friends took the only lift up."

Marco nods. "And your hotshot guys can't climb trees like the monkey-girl," he says, smiling slightly.

The agent grimaces. He curls his gloves into fists.

Elevator about to arrive at the landing, reports Jake in a hushed voice via Spy Link. **Are you still there? Hey, Marco?**

Marco swivels quickly to the console and uncovers the mike. "Yeah, I'm here," he says. "Listen, be advised that your situation is volatile. You read me? Stay on your toes, Bixby. Don't be stupid."

Roger that, replies Jake.

"And give me reports, like, every few seconds," adds Marco, glancing up at the Gloved Agent.

You got it, says Jake.

"And if you see some fairly nasty bald guys, possibly dressed like Carrolton Mall security, be smart and run, okay? Don't be afraid to scream and stuff."

Okay.

The Gloved Agent leans over Marco's shoulder, listening intently.

Marco glances up irritably. "Dude, could you stop breathing on me?"

The agent gives Marco a look meant to be chilling and inscrutable. Then, slowly, he leans back.

Team Spy Gear crouches, ready for action, as the turbo-lift rises through the opening in the wooden landing. But when they arrive, the landing is deserted.

Then Lexi looks up.

"Treehouses!" she gasps in awe.

The three boys are pretty astonished too. The lift landing where they arrive is a flat platform that sits beneath another structure, bigger and enclosed, just ten feet farther up Mother Nature's trunk. Like the landing, the structure above is built in a complete circle around the trunk. Even more amazing is a railed walkway extending from the side of the upper building. This stretches about fifty feet through the tree canopy to a similar building constructed around the trunk of the next huge Douglas fir! Beyond that, yet another walkway leads to a structure in a third tree.

"A treehouse *complex*!" utters Lucas.

Nearby, a solidly crafted staircase curves up Mother Nature's trunk from the lift's landing to an opening in the structure above.

"Let's go!" says Lexi, hopping over the lift railing.

"Whoa," whispers Jake. "You heard Marco. Let's move with some caution here." He looks around. "It's quiet," he reports to Marco. "I see no movement."

Okay, says Marco. **Good. Stay careful.**

Jake nods to Lucas, who presses another button on the lift's control panel. A section of the lift railing slides quietly open. Then the three boys step off and join Lexi at the foot of the curving stairs.

"Let me go first, kid," says Jake to Lexi. "And let's be stealthy, people."

Lexi looks disappointed but nods. Jake creeps up the stairs, and the others follow.

12

SECOND FLOOR

Slowly, Jake pokes his head through the opening at the top of the staircase. Then he looks down at Lucas, who crouches on the stairs just below him.

"Wow," whispers Jake.

"What?" Lucas asks. "What?"

Jake doesn't answer. He creeps up the last few steps through the opening. He looks around, then motions for the others to follow.

"Wow," says Lucas as he emerges.

He stands in a small curved corridor enclosed in thick Plexiglas. Directly ahead, at the opposite end of the short corridor, is a transparent, hatchlike door. The only thing on its smooth, clear surface is a black electronic keypad—no knobs, handles, or latches. On the inside curve of the corridor is Mother Nature's tree trunk, not quite as rotund as near the ground, but still massive. Through the glass on all other sides, Lucas sees a stunning high-tech laboratory filled with computer workstations and other gleaming instrumentation. The outer wall is solid white. Across the room, another glass door—with a simple doorknob, it appears, and no security keypad—leads out onto a catwalk.

Cyril climbs up into the corridor and looks around, nodding. He points through the glass. "Utterly sick and insane," he says.

Lexi, emerging behind him, says, "Intense."

"Extremely goats," adds Jake in agreement.

'Extremely goats' is not a report! calls Marco via Spy Link. **I want reports, Bixby.**

Jake carefully describes what he's seeing, then adds, "Dude, I have no idea what a quantum computer research lab looks like. But if I had to, like, *invent* one, this would be it."

Do you hear that? says Marco, as if to someone else. **Let's get them out of there.**

"What?" calls Jake.

Now muffled sounds and voices filter through static over the Spy Link.

"I can't hear you," says Jake. "Marco? Are you there? Marco!"

As Jake jabs a finger at his earpiece to hear better, Lucas steps past him toward the Plexiglas door. He looks at the black keypad. Its buttons are arranged in a three-by-four grid, the familiar pattern seen on telephones—numbered 1 through 9 plus keys for zero (0), pound (#), and star (*). Each numbered button from 2 through 9 has three letters of the alphabet associated with it: ABC with 2, DEF with 3, GHI with 4, and so on.

Lexi steps up next to him. Lucas punches in some random numbers. Six digits fill the keypad's digital display panel. Then the keypad buzzes and flashes a repeating message—two six-letter words, alternating ACCESS and DENIED.

"Hmmm," says Lucas. "It wants a six-number code."

"Or six letters," says Lexi, pointing at the flashing message.

They look at each other for a second.

Then, in unison, they say, "Victor."

Lucas quickly punches in the number sequence of the keys that spell VICTOR: 842867. The keypad emits a quiet, six-tone sequence.

The door hisses, then swings open.

"Yes!" replies Lucas.

Lucas bounces into the lab, which encircles the tree trunk. Lexi, Jake, and Cyril follow. Lucas approaches a large, enclosed glass case holding a contraption with tubes and gleaming metal cylinders and glowing red and green lights. He places his hand on the glass.

"I bet this is it," he says with reverence.

166

Lexi walks up beside him. "The quantum computer?" she asks.

"Yes," replies Lucas.

They stare at it for a second. "It looks like Christmas," says Lexi.

Lucas grins. "Christmas morning," he says. He looks up. "Hey, did you hear that beep?"

"It came from over there," says Lexi, pointing.

A shattered glass case hangs on the wall next to the outer exit door. Fragments of glass litter the floor beneath it. Something inside the case beeps again.

"Marco, what's going on?" asks Jake, still listening hard to his Spy Link.

Lucas and Lexi cross the room and examine the broken glass on the floor. Then Lucas looks closely at the panel inside the shattered case on the wall. Suddenly a light flashes on the panel. Lucas blinks and backs away, temporarily blinded.

Then a piercing siren sounds. It wails once, then stops.

A pleasant female voice emanates from speakers in the panel. "Iris scan complete. Self-destruct sequence triggered by intrusion alert," she says happily. "Self-destruct in five minutes. Please evacuate."

"Did she say . . . self-destruct?" asks Cyril.

Marco suddenly yells over the Spy Link channel. He shouts, Did you hear that?

More muffled sounds.

"Marco!" calls Jake.

Get out! screams Marco via Spy Link. **Now! Go! Run!**

And then the channel goes dead.

The heavy glass door hisses shut behind Team Spy Gear and the keypad display flashes two six-letter words, alternating: *EMGNCY* and *LOCKDN*. Cyril stares at the display.

"Emergency lockdown?" he guesses.

He pushes on the door. It doesn't move.

"Locked," he says, nodding. He smiles at Jake. "Trapped." He puts his hands in his pockets. "Doomed, would be my guess."

The siren blares again, then stops. Lucas rushes up to the keypad and punches in the VICTOR code again, but nothing happens. The display keeps flashing the red message, and the door remains locked.

Lucas slams his shoulder into the glass door.

"What the *dogs*?" he yells. "We can't get back to the lift!"

As if in response, the pleasant female voice says, "Emergency lockdown is in effect. Please exit the facility via the blue evacuation route."

Jake and Cyril exchange looks. Cyril shrugs.

"This is like a bad movie," he says.

Jake nods. "Say, you're remarkably calm," he says.

Cyril nods again. "Yes, I am, aren't I?" he answers. He starts whistling.

"Self-destruct in four minutes and thirty seconds," says

the happy female voice. "Please exit the facility via the blue evacuation route."

Jake glances across the lab at the exit door to the catwalk outside. His eyes widen as he spots something. He points at a small blue circle etched on the lab's white, antiseptic-looking outer wall.

"Blue route!" he says.

"Indeed it is," says Cyril. "Good find, lad."

"Let's go!" says Jake.

Leading the team, Jake rushes to the exit, but then stops so abruptly that Cyril runs into his back. Ahead, beyond the doorway, hangs a wood-slat suspension bridge. The railings on both sides are thick cables strung through metal struts attached to the floor slats at regular intervals. Jake spins to face the others.

"Does anybody here have a big problem with heights?" he calls out. "Like, a *big* problem?"

"Nope," says Cyril.

"Not me," says Lucas.

The boys look at Lexi. "Are you kidding?" she says.

"Okay, okay, good," says Jake, looking ill. "Because it's like, you know, we're, uh—"

"Really high up," Cyril finishes.

"Right."

"Four minutes until self-destruct," says the voice. "Please proceed to the blue evacuation route in a brisk and orderly manner. And have a nice day."

Jake just stands in the doorway.

"Jake," says Cyril casually. "Maybe we should, like, escape?"

"Right," says Jake.

Lucas, surprised, steps up to his brother. "You're afraid of heights?"

"Yes."

"Why don't I know this?" asks Lucas. "I mean, I'm your brother."

"I've never been this high before," says Jake. "Ever."

Cyril claps Jake on the shoulder. "I'll take point, bud," he says.

Jake nods and steps aside. Cyril edges past him through the doorway. As he steps out onto the catwalk, he glances down. "Whoa," he says. "Jake, keep your eyes on my hair. Got it?"

"Got it," says Jake weakly.

"Eyes on my hair!" repeats Cyril loudly.

"Okay, got it."

Dramatically, Cyril throws his arm forward. "Move out, troop!" he calls in a deep voice.

Just as they move forward, the Spy Link channel clicks back on. Static crackles. "Marco, is that you?" calls Lucas. "Do you read me, over?"

For a second there is silence. Then a strange voice speaks. It sounds like a small man in desperate need of Kleenex.

Commence *immediate* evacuation, says the voice urgently. Ride the lift down with all possible speed. You are in *extreme* danger.

"Who's that?" demands Lucas, looking around at the others on the catwalk. "Who are you? Where's Marco?"

Bring the lift down now! says the voice.

"We can't!" says Lucas.

Why not? whines the nasal voice.

"Because the door's locked, and who the donkey are you?" asks Cyril.

More static. Then silence.

"Three minutes until self-destruct," says the female voice, echoing strangely from speakers somewhere in the trees. "Please exit the facility via the blue evacuation route."

Cyril looks up into the branches.

"I hate that woman," he says.

The catwalk leads to a second circular structure, roughly the same size as the lab but with more windows and a balcony. Cyril steps onto the balcony from the catwalk and looks around.

"Follow the balcony!" calls Lucas.

The polished wood balcony curves around the structure in either direction from the door. Cyril heads left. When he reaches the first window, he peeks inside. "Living quarters," he says.

Indeed, the room is a comfortable lounge with black leather sofas and chairs. A blond oak breakfast bar with several stools separates the lounge from a kitchen area. As the team hurries around the curve of the balcony, Cyril glances into the next window. This looks in on another room—a warmly lit study, complete with ceiling-high bookshelves and a large rolltop desk with a green-shaded banker's lamp. Expensive-looking art hangs on the wall too. Just around the tree trunk that rises up through the room's center, Cyril can see that a door on the opposite wall is wide open.

He is about to move on, but something familiar catches his eye on the desktop. In a split second he whips Spy Nightscope binoculars out of a side pouch of his cargo pants and trains them on the desktop.

"What are you doing?" says Lucas. "Let's go!"

"What are you looking at?" asks Jake, who feels a bit less acrophobic on the wide balcony.

Cyril, gazing through the scope, drops his jaw.

"You won't believe this," he says.

"What?"

Cyril lowers the scope. He turns to Lucas and says, "Dude, photocopies of your Spy Gear casebook are spread all over that desk." He points. "See? That's the cover, right on top." He looks through the scope again. "There's some kind of security badge with a photo ID lying on top, but I can make out some of your gadget sketches."

Lucas grabs the Spy Nightscope and looks. He's stunned. "Who copied my notes?" He tries to zoom in on the photo ID on the security badge.

The pleasant security voice says, "Self-destruct in two minutes, thirty seconds."

"Let's discuss it a little later, okay, guys?" pleads Lexi.

Cyril shakes his head and moves on. "This is insanely deranged," he says.

The foursome rounds the curve to the opposite side of the building, where two more narrow catwalks connect to the balcony. Each one extends to a different tree.

"Great!" says Cyril. "A fork in the path." He slaps his forehead and looks around. "Yet another cheesy action-adventure cliché."

"Which way do we go?" pants Lucas.

Jake, who has been very quiet and moving stiffly, takes a deep breath and says, "That way." He points to another blue circle emblazoned on the balcony near the rightmost catwalk.

"Ah, the blue route," says Cyril.

They hurry across the catwalk, which runs to a small roofless platform; it resembles the lift-landing back on Mother Nature. And sure enough, when the kids round the platform to the far side of the tree, they find another track embedded in the trunk, identical to the first one. It runs both up and down.

But the lift is nowhere to be seen. When Lucas approaches the control panel next to the track, he finds a message flashing:

SECURITY EMERGENCY:
SYSTEMS LOCKDOWN

He starts punching buttons. Suddenly, a siren wails directly above their heads!

"Nothing is working!" he shouts above the siren's wail.

"Who planned this stupid blue route?" yells Cyril.

"No, it's over there!" calls Lexi. She points at a small hatch in the platform floor. A blue circle is etched in its wood.

The siren stops wailing.

"Self-destruct in two minutes," says the recorded female voice.

"Shut the heck up!" shouts Cyril.

Lexi looks nervous now. "Are we gonna blow up?" she asks.

"No," says Jake firmly, moving toward the floor hatch.

"Why?"

"Because it's too crazy," says Jake. "Up this high, people would see it for fifty miles around." He pulls open the hatch. "Viper is all about deep cover and stealth. I can't believe he'd just blow stuff up."

Cyril nods. "It doesn't make sense that he would just, you know, turn Mother Nature into a two-hundred-foot-tall Roman candle." He thinks about this for a moment. "Although that would be pretty cool."

Lucas looks around. "So what's this countdown all about?" he asks.

Jake gives his brother an honest look. "I don't know," he says, then stares down at the opening beneath the floor hatch. "And what the monkey is this?"

Lucas slides next to Jake to see a round Plexiglas cover blocking the hole under the wooden hatch. This one has a slim digital keypad built in. Under the clear glass, a bluish tube drops straight down, then spirals out of sight around the tree trunk.

"Wow," says Lucas. "It looks like the most amazing playground twisty slide you could ever imagine."

Cyril looks over his shoulder. "Demented!" he says with admiration.

"And it looks like we need another code," adds Lucas. He glances up at Lexi. "Anything come to mind? Anything at all?"

Lexi shrugs. "Nope."

"Self-destruct in ninety seconds," says the voice. "Please exit the facility to the blue evacuation point and enter the six-digit evacuation code, which can be found on the back of your security clearance badge."

All four members of Team Spy Gear stare up at the voice.

"Great," says Jake.

He exchanges a look with Cyril.

"I'll go," says Cyril. "The door was open back there."

"No, I'm faster," Lucas protests.

"I can't argue with that," says Cyril.

With a deep breath, Lucas bursts into action. He sprints

across the catwalk to the second building, breathing hard and trying not to look down. He veers left on the balcony, runs to the open door, and hurries inside to the rolltop desk. Quickly, he nabs the security card, pauses a second, looking at his copied casebook notes, then grins and nabs them, too.

"Self-destruct in sixty seconds," reports the female voice.

Then Lucas sprints back to the team.

As he arrives, he finds them all staring up the trunk of the tree.

"I got it!" he shouts, holding up the badge. "What are you looking at?"

"The lift is coming down," says Lexi, pointing up the silver track in the trunk.

Sure enough, the bottom of the lift appears through the branches, dropping slowly. As the foursome watch nervously, a shaven head appears over the edge, glaring down at them.

"Crud!" yells Jake. "Lucas—"

But Lucas is already reading the code number etched in blue on the back of the security badge, then punching it into the digital keypad. The Plexiglas cover slides open with a hiss.

"Down the hatch!" shouts Jake.

Lexi, grinning wildly, hops feetfirst into the escape tube below. The boys hear her squeals of delight as she rides the blue spiral down.

"Hurry!" calls Jake, staring up at the lift.

"Thirty seconds to self-destruct," says the voice.

And then the lift stops. It stays motionless for a couple of seconds . . . and then reverses direction, heading back upward. Suddenly, a mechanical whine can be heard somewhere above—powerful, like a jet engine, but quieter. It's a familiar sound to the Spy Gear team. And then the pine branches start shaking. They can feel the growing downdraft.

"Viper's spaceship!" hollers Cyril.

"Go, Lucas!" shouts Jake.

Lucas hops into the tube and disappears below around the first curve of the spiral. Cyril gulps, looks at Jake, and leaps in next. He yells, "Geronimo!"

Jake sits down and lowers his legs into the tube. Before he lets go of the edge, however, he stares back up into the darkened branches. They shudder wildly now in the violent, whining airflow of the hovercraft above. Through the shuddering crosshatch of limbs, he catches glimpses of multicolored lights. Jake's last crazy thought as he lets himself plummet is how much it looks like a holiday display up there.

Then into the tube he goes, spiraling downward at the speed of blue light.

(13)

HOLIDAY ON ICE

Half an hour later, Team Spy Gear troops down Agincourt Drive.

Light snow is falling. It just started a few minutes ago. The low clouds promising winter for days have finally opened for business.

Cyril walks with a limp. He shakes his head. "Why would they put an inverted twist in an emergency escape slide?" he asks.

"For fun?" suggests Lexi.

Lucas Bixby is rubbing his tailbone. "I'm pretty sure it's a centrifugal velocity brake," he says.

"Yeah, you really come screaming around that last loop pretty fast," agrees Jake Bixby, who, now that we notice, is walking kind of funny too. "I guess it's supposed to slow you down."

"Whatever," says Cyril.

"I thought it was fun!" Lexi says.

Cyril gives her a sour look. But then he stops short, gazing past her. A hideously monstrous shadow figure looms in the trees across the street.

"Don't you answer your phone?" Cyril calls out to the fiend.

Marco steps out of the shadows. He shrugs.

"Why didn't you answer your Spy Link?" asks Jake. "We called you, like, a zillion times."

"They shut it down," says Marco.

"Shut down the Spy Link?" asks Jake.

"They shut down Stoneship."

There is a tense pause. Then:

"What?" shouts Lucas, looking stricken. "Who? Who shut it down?"

"Some little self-important dude from the Agency," says Marco with a hint of anger. "They wouldn't let me contact you." He digs his fingers into his dreadlocks and rubs his scalp. "I tried, but some of his boys had me pretty good by the hair."

Lucas, still crestfallen, approaches Marco.

"So, like, we can't go back up there?" he asks. "I mean, what about all our stuff?"

Jake pats his brother on the shoulder. "It's not *our* stuff, bro," he says.

"Why not?" blurts Lucas. He slings the gadget

backpack off his back and hugs it close to his chest.

"Chill, dude," says Marco. A hint of amusement crosses his face. "You can keep your stuff."

"But Stoneship," says Lucas. He tries to speak, but can't for a second. Finally, he says, "I *love* that place."

Marco folds his huge grizzly arms across his chest. "You're misunderstanding me," he says. "You can still go to Stoneship."

"So he *didn't* shut it down?"

"No, *he* did," nods Marco. "But then someone much bigger overruled him."

"Who?"

"Him." Marco points down the street. The team turns to look. Another huge dark figure—huger than Marco even—stands silhouetted by a streetlamp's warm glow. He raises a hand—it looks like a bear paw—and then quickly steps into an idling black BMW sedan. They watch as he cruises off.

"The Dark Man," says Cyril, eyes wide.

"He wants to meet you," says Marco.

"Us?"

"Yes," says Marco. "You. Hard to believe, isn't it?"

"When?" says Jake.

"Soon," says Marco. "Very soon."

Marco quickly briefs Team Spy Gear on his Stoneship encounters with the Gloved Agent. Then he adds, "But our big dark friend likes your work. Although it kind of irritates him that you're doing better than his guys."

Jake looks over at Marco. "We saw Viper's airship again," he says.

"Yep."

"And then we saw the black helicopters arrive," says Lucas.

"Yeah, about two minutes too late, as usual," says Marco.

"Did they find anything interesting?" asks Jake.

"Yes," nods Marco. "They found a quantum computer prototype, totally fried." He gives Jake a serious look. "And very, very hot."

"Hot?"

"There was a release of radioactive energy triggered by the self-destruct," explains Marco. "Confined to the lab, which was built to contain it. But seriously unhealthy. Lethal, even." He shakes his head with disgust. "It was an unacceptably dangerous situation."

This silences everyone for a few seconds.

Then Marco looks at Cyril. He says, "But you got out okay."

"Yeah, we rode a tube," says Cyril. "And shot out into a blinking evergreen bush at about *eighty miles an hour.*"

"Cool," says Marco.

Lucas still looks a little down. "So we failed," he says.

"What?" says Marco. "Are you kidding? You dogs are heroes. Again."

"How?"

"Who found the lab in the first place?" asks Marco.

Lexi raises her hand. Marco rolls his eyes.

"Yes?" he says.

Lexi says, "Um, we did."

"Very good," says Marco. "You get a puppy sticker."

"Really?" asks Lexi.

"No!" shouts Marco.

Then something else strikes Jake, and he frowns. "What about the mole?" he asks.

"What about him?" says Marco.

"Where is he?" asks Jake.

"Chatting with Viper right now, I expect."

"Dang," says Lucas. "So, like, we didn't actually rescue him or anything."

"You weren't supposed to," says Marco. "They still want him working on the inside."

"Who is he?" asks Jake.

"I don't have that information," says Marco with a quick nervous glance at the spot where the Dark Man stood.

Jake notices and nods. "Cool," he says.

Marco lowers his voice significantly. "But I would guess he's a big tool in Viper's quantum project. In fact, he might even be a bald-headed honcho." Marco gives Jake a look. "This is just speculation, of course."

Jake frowns again. "So then . . . what's to stop Viper from whipping up a new quantum computer?"

Marco shakes a cloud of snowflakes from his mop of dreadlocks. "The technology is fragile," he says. "It's primitive. We have six months, maybe more, until they can build and calibrate a new operational prototype. By then maybe we'll have a counterunit." He grins and his eyes grow intense with pleasure. "I picture myself at the keyboard."

"Or better yet, maybe somebody will actually catch Viper by then," says Jake.

Marco shakes his head. "Not a chance," he says. "He's too smart for these guys."

"Okay, so maybe we'll catch Viper for them," says Jake with a grim smile.

Marco laughs. "Well, without you children doing the fieldwork and deciphering all the clues, the Agency would be chasing biting blackflies in Saskatchewan right now."

"So gee whiz, golly, we *did* sort of save the world here, fellas," says Cyril. "Even though it doesn't actually *feel* like it right now."

"Viper's not blasting past firewalls and hacking out national security data," Lucas agrees. "Or disrupting the international banking system. Or taking over missile guidance systems and blowing up stuff."

"So it's all good!" says Lexi.

"For now," says Jake.

"Yes," says Marco. "For now."

Suddenly, Cyril's cell phone rings. The ring tone plays the opening bars of "White Christmas." He flips open the phone and says, "Hello? Oh, huh, hey." He lowers his voice significantly. "'Sup, Cat?"

Jake and Lucas exchange a look.

"Ice skating?" says Cyril. "Downtown?"

He looks over at Jake. Jake grins big. Most of the teeth are visible in this particular species of grin.

"Uh, sure, sure," says Cyril. "Tonight. Yeah, it is Saturday after all, isn't it? Yes. We can be there. See ya."

"We?" says Jake, frowning.

Grinning now, Cyril flips his phone shut with the Click of Finality. "She has a friend," he says slyly.

Jake swallows. "A friend?"

"Yes. A friend." Cyril raises his eyebrows. *"A friend who wants to meet this Bixby fellow."*

Jake cannot speak.

Marco stretches. "Wow. Think I'll head back to my grunge pit and get some sleep," he says.

Lucas and Lexi, fighting back snickers and guffaws, suddenly take off jogging up the street. "We gotta go!" shoots Lucas over his shoulder. "Big school project. Much work to be done. Adios, bro!"

Jake just keeps standing there with his mouth hanging open.

Cyril nods at him.

"Come on, dog," he says. "This should be interesting.

I've never skated before." He crooks his arm around Jake's neck. "Fortunately, I'm such a finely tuned athlete that I'm sure I'll pick it up with *amazing* alacrity."

Stunned, Jake says, "Do you think we'll, you know, play some hockey with these girls?"

"No, Jake," says Cyril. "No hockey."

"We'll race them, right?"

"No racing," says Cyril. "No, I'm sure we'll just skate arm in arm with them, going around and around in circles, around and around and around, singing Christmas carols and laughing like idiots." He nods. "It will be *so much fun*."

Jake looks ill. "I don't know, Cyril," he says. "I don't think I'm ready. . . ."

"Look," says Cyril insistently. "You just saved the world. You just walked a series of catwalks a hundred and fifty feet up in the sky." He grabs Jake by the shoulders and looks him in the eye. "You can *do* this, son."

After a few more seconds of staring, Jake nods.

"Okay," he says. "I can do this."

"You can do this!"

"Yes, I can do this."

And thus we pull the sat-cam back, back up into the sky. Flakes fall faintly, faintly falling like little white specks of frozen crystallized water, which, amazingly enough, is exactly what they are. If that doesn't amaze you, I don't know what will. And back we go, even farther. Look, there's the frozen ice rink, right there, downtown, conveniently located just a block from the Hot Chocolate Shoppe! A coincidence like that should restore your faith in a universe aligned with Good Things.

Just look at Carrolton, will you?

How do they get so many lights up in one place? Who comes up with that many colors? It's amazing, is what it is.

And if you can look down on all those kids in goofy mittens and the lights and the bells of holiday carols and still have sour eyes and feel disgust, then I feel sorry for you. There's just no excuse for that kind of attitude, mister.

Even if you're named after a snake.

Turn the page for a Sneak Peek at . . .

ADVENTURES

THE DOOMSDAY DUST

1

THE BALD SPOT

Carrolton is a great place to live, but let's be honest. In January, the place is *ridiculously freaking* cold.

See it down there? It's that sleepy suburban dot in the middle of the big white region.

Zoom in on the white region.

Okay, that's snow, mostly, except for up there in Chimichanga County, which is entirely covered in baking soda. You Chimichanga kids can test this by dumping a gallon of vinegar outside. Watch the chemical reaction. Fun! This is also a good way to clean dirty coins, by the way.

But let's not lose our focus so early in the book. Rather, let's do a quick comparison. Kids, pan your satellite view south to those green areas near the equator. See them? Those are tropical forests and whatnot. It's warm there in late January—hot, even.

But Carrolton is white and cold.

Scan back north to Carrolton and then zoom in a bit more. See?

The Carrolton reservoir is rock hard. Nearby, Black-water Creek trickles under a glaze of ice. Downtown in the business district, the city pond is a polished diamond and teeming with ice skaters. Everything's frozen solid. Bitter winds howl from the north, and snow covers everything.

But here's the bizarre thing: Carrolton kids like it this way.

Because when things freeze, everything gets really slick.

By the way, *where* have you been?

Seriously, I like most of you guys, but do you really expect me to keep an eye on Carrolton all by myself? Sure, I'm the author, but I can't keep track of everything. Especially from my office up here on the International Space Station.[1]

Anyway, since you've been gone, strange things have been happening in this quiet, happy town. First, let's examine the phenomenon I've been tracking most care-fully during your irresponsible absence. Please pan your satellite cameras to the south edge of Stoneship Woods. Zoom down close. Note how the northern wind rushes

---

1 Kids, please don't tell NASA I'm here.

through the trees, scattering and twirling the dry snow. As each gust wanes, the white whirlwinds settle back into the snowscape.

Uh, except for those two.

Over there.

See them? Near the bridge where Ridgeview Drive crosses over Blackwater Creek? Right there: two white whirlwinds, each about three feet high. Both hover above the dark creek ice . . . and continue doing so even after the wind dies.

In fact, they pulse up and down as if alive.

And now things get even more interesting.

Suddenly, a long black sedan roars up Ridgeview Drive. As it passes over the creek bridge, its driver slams on the brakes. The car skids wildly, swerving sideways. The doors burst open before the vehicle even halts. Four men in black suits and dark sunglasses leap out.

Down in the creek, the two wispy whirlwinds start circling each other.

They look nervous.

One of the black-suited agents slings a heavy-looking tank onto his back as he emerges from the car. A hose runs from the tank to a suction tube that the man holds in one hand. He flicks a switch on the tube's handle and the tank suddenly whines loudly. It sounds like, well, a vacuum cleaner.

Meanwhile, the other black-suited men hop off the bridge into a snow bank along the creek. The man with the vacuum cleaner follows, fighting to keep his balance as he staggers. Out on the ice the white whirlwinds continue to pulse up and down, as if in confusion. The four agents approach the strange entities cautiously; they creep within twenty feet. Ten feet.

At five feet, they stop. Nobody moves.

The whirlwinds seem to appraise the men for a few seconds. And vice versa.

Then the agent wearing the vacuum tank takes a slow step to the very edge of the ice. And with an abrupt, violent thrust he jabs the suction tube into the nearest of the two whirlwinds. Within seconds, the white swirl disappears, its particles sucked from the air into the tank.

The other whirlwind starts pulsing wildly, almost violently. It changes colors from white to black, then back to white, then black again. It floats several feet up the creek, but does not flee. Suddenly, it rushes directly at the three other agents! It flows around them, over them, zooming back and forth among them. The three agents flap their hands and fan their arms at the swirling black dust, trying to drive it away. Soon, all three men are coughing violently.

The man with the vacuum tank keeps trying to jab the suction tube at the renegade entity, but the thing is lightning fast. After a few seconds it darts back out over the frozen creek. Then, suddenly, its particles collapse, dropping straight down to form a flat black circle on the ice.

The tank-wearing agent tries to jab the suction tube at this scattering. But he's too far away. He takes a tentative step out onto the creek ice. Then another. The ice holds. One more step, and he's close enough to the whirlwind's resting place.

But as tank-man carefully extends the suction tube down toward the black circle, the entity abruptly rises again, hissing loudly—this time in a jagged, amorphous, hostile-looking shape. It flashes silver, then angry red. The agent leaps backward in fear. *Crack!*

For a second the man stands motionless.

Crack! Crack!

Then he falls through the ice.

The dust entity quickly reforms into a white whirlwind and escapes with stunning speed up the creek. Within mere seconds it darts around a bend.

Fortunately for the agent with the vacuum tank, Blackwater Creek is very shallow this time of year; he stands only knee-deep in the frigid water. The other three agents, still coughing, scramble toward him to help.

Okay, that's some weird, wacky stuff right there, my friends.

Now pull back and pan up to the northern edge of Stoneship Woods.

Center your focus on those really tall, old trees. That's the Old North Stand, where the last Spy Gear Adventure more or less ended. Remember? If you don't, that's okay. Just grab one of your copies of *The Quantum Quandary* and reread it several times until you've got it mostly memorized. Then throw it in the trash because you messed it up by getting fingerprints on it and whatnot. Go to the bookstore and buy a few more fresh copies with your parents' hard-earned money, knowing that it's going to a good cause.[2]

Scan farther north just across Ridgeview Drive, then a little west toward Blackwater Creek.

See that pond next to the creek bed?

That's not a pond, actually. Rather, it's a shallow depression in the open space known as the Bald Spot. Weeks ago, somebody flooded it with creek water. Now the Bald Spot is a big ice rink.

Hey, look. Two boys are walking down Agincourt Drive, which curves past the Bald Spot. They both wear big ski coats and caps. Both carry broomball sticks. Both are brothers—coincidentally, to each other. Indeed, both are named Bixby.

Let's follow them.

As these Bixby brothers approach the ice, a skinny, thirteen-year-old kid wearing a Siberian sheepskin tundra hat with fur earflaps turns to them. He holds a plastic ball in one hand and a broomball stick in the other. Massive shoots of hair explode like black icicles from beneath his hat. The earflaps flop loosely as the lad raises his stick in salute.

"Greetings, men of Bixby!" he intones in his deepest voice.

The Bixby boys raise their sticks in reply.

"Cyril!" Jake calls out. "Out of the doghouse, I see."

"Somewhat, yes," nods Cyril. "Mother no longer hisses or spits at the sight of me."

"So how is it that you're here?"

"Dude, I wouldn't miss this game for anything."

"I understand that," says Jake. "But if you're grounded, how can you—"

"I bribed her."

Jake says, "So, like, you promised to take out the trash for the next month or something?"

"No," says Cyril. "Actually, I gave her a hundred dollars."

Jake nods. "You bought your freedom for a hundred dollars."

"That's correct, Jake."

"Because you love broomball."

"Deeply."

Lucas smirks. "But you stink at broomball."

"But I love it."

Jake gives him a sly look. "How about if I give you a hundred bucks to go home right now?"

"It's a deal!" yells Cyril.

He whips off his glove and reaches out his hand, but the two fellows laugh like jackals and undergo a complex Western greeting ritual known as a "handshake." After a hand clasp, a few spins, and some knuckle punches, they flutter their fingers at each other and end it with a two-finger pointing gesture.

Cyril Wong has been Jake's best friend ever since the Jurassic era. He's quite skinny, and kind of rubbery too. Those of you who know Cyril from previous Spy Gear Adventures know about his hyper-serious, scholarly demeanor. The kid has no sense of humor. It's too bad, really.

Suddenly, a small dark-eyed waif wearing a purple stocking cap and a huge, blue down vest skids up next to the boys. Long strands of black hair hang from her cap and flutter in the breeze.

"Avast, dog," says the girl. She looks at Lucas and raises her stick.

"Yo Lexter!" grins Lucas. He raises his stick too.

They clack the sticks together multiple times. Then they both bow.

Lexi Lopez, eleven, is Lucas Bixby's best friend. She's also the best gymnast in town. Plus she's made almost entirely of molecules. As a result, Lexi looks very interesting under an electron microscope. One other thing: She's the star of the broomball team.

Cyril taps the ice with his stick and turns to Lucas. "I

must say, young Bixby, you've done it again, chap." He drops the ball to the rink then rears back and whacks it violently with his stick. "The ice is perfect, my man."

"He's a mechanical genius, as you well know," nods Jake.

"It's even better than last year's ice," calls Lexi as she scoots after the ball.

Lucas grins.

One year ago, using just a few common household items— a leaf blower, some garden hoses, two desk clamps, and a Yakmar XE 1300-watt industrial-grade plutonium-rod power generator—Lucas Bixby managed to rig up a crude siphon pump. He used this pump to suck water from Black-water Creek and spew it into the Bald Spot depression, flooding the central area three inches deep.

It being January in Carrolton, the water froze solid within forty-eight hours.

Once the ice was solid, Jake and Lucas put up a pair of four-by-six goals, and then rounded up Cyril, Lexi, and other neighborhood kids for some broomball madness. Word spread. Soon dozens of kids were scurrying over the ice with sticks every day after school, whacking at blue rubber broomballs with joyful abandon.

Indeed, attendance grew so fast that Lucas had to reassemble his siphon pump, hammer another hole in the crystal crust of Blackwater Creek, and flood the Bald

Spot still deeper so the iced area grew. Kids set up a second rink. Within weeks an informal league formed. Soon the league became more formal—believe it or not, organized by kids *with no parental involvement whatsoever*!

Of course, when Jake had first proposed such heresy, Lucas was stunned.

"But who will yell at us?" he asked. "I mean, how can we possibly hope to compete at sports without adults to belittle us into achieving excellence?"

"Good point," nodded Jake. "I don't know. I guess we'll have to play for fun."

"Fun?" scoffed Lucas. "What kind of motivation is *fun*?" He tried to blink confusion from his eyes. "I mean, how can we build character without overcoming gut-wrenching adversity? Jake, we need adult coaches to yell at us, or we aren't *learning* anything."

Now, one year later, in deepest winter, this Bixby-created broomball arena has become the center of the Carrolton Kid World.

Today Team Spy Gear faces a tough match against the Black Dogs, a team of kids from the Willow Estates neighborhood in the south part of town. Unfortunately, our flashback to last year forced us to miss the first six minutes of the game. The score is 2-1 already, with Team Spy Gear in the lead. You also missed the three cows that ran mooing across the field, plus the Allosaurus that was chasing them. Plus the comet. You missed that, too.

Next time you read this chapter, you might want to just skip the flashback.

Anyhow, it's a pretty good game so far.

Right now, Jake is playing defense. He poke-checks the ball from an attacking Black Dog, then swats it forward to Lexi. After a nifty step-over move, she slides the ball across the ice to Lucas who is flying down the left wing. Lucas gathers the ball and holds it just long enough to draw two defensemen, then he slaps it backward to Jake who trails the play.

Now Jake has a wide-open look from about twenty feet.

Grinning with glee, he takes a full windup and slaps a screaming missile at the goal. Unfortunately, it sails high. The goalie punches the ball higher still as it sails over him.

The ball caroms out of the rink. It skitters down a snow bank toward Blackwater Creek.

"Dang it!" yells the goalie.

"It's okay—I got it!" calls Lucas.

He scoots off the ice and tromps through calf-deep snow, then scrambles down the creek bank. The ball sits like a big blue fruit just inches from the ice. Relieved, Lucas approaches the blue sphere. But something catches his eye.

Just down the creek, maybe thirty yards away, a small flock of birds circles in a tight formation. They look like black sparrows; they circle a spot just three feet above the frozen surface of the ice.

Mesmerized, Lucas trudges a few steps closer.

The flock's circling motion is fast and follows an oddly regular pattern. Indeed, as Lucas approaches, the black birds speed up. Soon their movement is nearly a blur, so fast it seems a miracle they don't collide.

"That's so sick!" whispers Lucas in awe.

These birds are incredible! He reaches a patch of brittle, neck-high cattails jutting from the snow. As Lucas edges forward, he uses his broomball stick to push aside reeds. When he finally emerges from the cattails, he frowns.

Up close, the birds are . . . white?

How could that be?

The flock notices him now and moves away, up the creek. Strangely, however, it continues circling near the ground. Lucas watches in wonder. When the birds near the next bend, they drop even lower. The precision of their swirling pattern is mind-boggling.

Then the birds evaporate into white dust.

Lucas blinks.

The birds are gone.